Erotic Zombies
A Twisted Eerie Thriller

Erotic Zombies
A Twisted Eerie Thriller

BY

TRACY WILSON

http://beautifulpublications.com

Published by
Beautiful Publications LLC
Stratford, CT 06614

PRINT ISBN: 978-1-7343352-6-2
EBOOK ISBN: 978-1-7343352-7-9

Printed in the United States of America

"Good morning – thanks for coming in..." Jay's teacher said as we walked into the classroom...

"This is nice – I bet Jay has a lot of fun in here..." Bazil said as he walked over to the play area with the colorful mat and looked around...

"He certainly does... but that's not why I called you..."

"Ms. Shelby... is Jay giving you a problem?" I asked as I sat down beside her...

"Mr. Osgood... please join us..."

"Of course..." Bazil said as he came over and sat in the chair beside me...

"I don't know how to say this..." Ms. Shelby sighed... "So I'm just going to say it..."

"Say what?" Bazil asked...

"Ummm... is your bedroom close to Jay's room?"

"Why are you asking about our bedroom?" I laughed...

"Well... the other day... Jay made this picture..." she answered as she took a picture out of her desk and showed it to us...

"Oh shit!" Bazil laughed. Jay drew a picture of a bed with two stick figures – one on top of the other... and at the opposite end of the paper... Jay colored some grass with two stick figures – one on top of the other – but the difference was these stick figures, had scary faces...

"When I asked Jay about the picture... he told me this was you... and these are the monsters..."

"Monsters?" I repeated...

"Yes..."

"Ms. Shelby... are you saying our son sees us as monsters?" Bazil asked, raising his voice...

"Mr. Osgood... please..."

"I'm sorry – I didn't mean to raise my voice..."

"I think what's going on here is that maybe he wakes up in the middle of the night and he's not sure what's going on... and it scares him..."

"Is that what he told you?" I asked...

"Not exactly..."

"What did he tell you... exactly?" Bazil asked...

"He said Mommy and Daddy play in their room and the monsters play outside..."

"Wait – we play in our room and the monsters play outside? Outside where?" I asked...

"Jay said the monsters play outside in the backyard... when it's dark..."

"Can we keep this?" Bazil asked as he picked up the picture...

"Sure..."

"We're going to talk to our son..." Bazil said as he got up to leave...

"Mr. Osgood... I'm sorry..."

"No apologies necessary – c'mon Beautiee – let's go..." Bazil said as he started walking towards the door...

"Thank you Ms. Shelby..." I said as I got up to leave and walked out the door behind Bazil...

"Come here..." he said and then he pulled me into a kiss...

"Bazil..."

"Beautiee – please tell me you don't believe Jay thinks we're monsters..."

"Hell no!" I exclaimed...

"Okay then – let's go home and talk to our son..."

"I wonder if he's being bullied..."

"I don't think so..." Bazil said as we got in the car and headed home. When we got home they couldn't wait for us to get out of the car...

"Mommy! Daddy! You're home!"

"Wait a damn minute!" Keisha laughed as she opened the door and they ran up to us...

"Hi Daddy! I got a good report right Daddy?" Jay squealed...

"Me too – right Daddy?" Joseph squealed...

"Me too – right Auntie Keisha?" Joy squealed...

"Yes Joy – you were good..." she answered...

"Yeeaaa!"

"Keisha – could you take Joseph and Jay to your house for a few minutes?" Bazil asked... "We need to talk to Jay..."

"Can I go?" Jay asked...

"No Jay – come over here to Mommy..." I said as I picked him up...

"C'mon y'all..." Keisha said as she took the kids by the hand and walked them over to her house and we went inside with Jay...

"Daddy - are you mad at me?" Jay asked with tears in his eyes..."

"Nope..." Bazil answered as we went into the kitchen. I had no idea what Bazil was up to until we all sat at the table... "Jay?"

"Yes Daddy?"

"You want some ice cream?"

"Yeea!"

"Okay – but it's a secret..." Bazil said as he went over to the cabinet and took down 3 bowls. Jay kicked his feet back and forth in the chair as Bazil went in the refrigerator, took out the vanilla ice cream, made the three bowls, and brought them to the table...

"Thank you Daddy!" Jay squealed as he started eating the ice cream...

"Remember – it's a secret – okay?"

"Okay Daddy!" he beamed and then he went back to eating his ice cream...

"Jay... do you like school?" Bazil asked as we started eating too...

"Uh huh..." Jay answered with a spoonful of ice cream in his mouth...

"Do you have a lot of friends?"

"Uh huh..." Jay answered again...

"Who's your best friend?"

"Charles..."

"Is he in your class?"

"Uh huh..." Jay answered as we finished our ice cream...

"Jay – I need to ask you something... and I need you to tell me the truth – okay?"

"Yes Daddy..."

"Do you know what this is?" Bazil asked as he took the paper out of his pocket, unfolded it, and put it on the table in front of Jay...

"My picture!" Jay beamed...

"Who's this?" Bazil asked as he pointed to the stick figures in the bed...

"That's you – and that's Mommy..."

"What are we doing?"

"You're playing..." Jay laughed...

"Who are they?" Bazil asked as he pointed to the other stick figures...

"The monsters..."

"What are they doing?"

"They're playing..." Jay sighed...

"Jay... are you scared of the monsters?"

"Uh huh..." he sniffed as he started crying...

"Come here..." Bazil said as he picked Jay up and held him... "Daddy's gonna make the monsters go away so you don't have to be scared... okay?"

"Okay Daddy..." Jay sniffed...

"Can you show me where the monsters play?" Bazil asked as he stood up and went towards the French doors...

"I'm scared Daddy..." Jay said as he wrapped his arms around Bazil's neck...

"I gotchu..." Bazil said. Bazil stood by the French doors but didn't open them. I saw Jay trembling in Bazil's arms and I went to take him from Bazil but he stopped me... "Jay... Daddy's gonna make the monsters go away... but I need your help... can you help Daddy?"

"Okay..." Jay sniffed as Bazil opened the French doors slowly...

"You okay Jay?"

"Uh huh..." Bazil stepped outside and looked around...

"Hmmm... I don't see any monsters..."

"They come when it's dark..." Jay whispered...

"Show Daddy where the monsters come..."

"Right there..." Jay whispered as he pointed to the area behind the pool...

"Okay Jay – you go with Mommy – I'll be right back..."

"Daddy – Nooo...."

"C'mon Jay – I said as I took Jay in my arms...

"I want Daddy!" Jay cried...

"Daddy's okay Jay... he's right there... see?" I said as I pointed out into the backyard. I watched as Bazil stood there looking around and then he came back into the kitchen, closed the French doors, and locked them...

"Come sit down Jay..." Bazil said as he took Jay from me and sat him in the chair...

"Did you make the monsters go away Daddy?"

"Not yet... but we can do it together..."

"I'm scared Daddy..."

"You don't have to be scared anymore... but I need your help..."

"Okay Daddy..."

"You said the monsters come out at night – right?"

"Uh huh..."

"Do you remember the first time you saw the monsters?"

"Uh huh..."

"What happened?"

"I heard the monsters..."

"You heard them?"

"Uh huh..."

"Come on Jay – let's go upstairs to your room..." Bazil said as he picked Jay up and I followed them upstairs to the boys' room... "Jay – show Daddy where you saw the monsters..." Bazil said...

"Over there..." Jay said as he pointed towards the window. Bazil took Jay over to the window and looked down into the yard...

"Thank you for helping Daddy..." Bazil said as he walked away from the window...

"You're welcome Daddy..."

"I need you to do something for me..."

"Okay Daddy..."

"Tonight – I want you to come get me when you see the monsters – okay?"

"Okay Daddy..."

"C'mon – we're going to get your brother and your sister..." Bazil said as we walked out the room and headed down the hallway towards the stairs...

"Daddy?"

"Yes Jay?"

"Please don't let the monsters get my brother or my sister..." he said as he started tearing up...

"They won't get any of us... I promise..."

"Okay Daddy..."

"I need you to do something for me..."

"Yes Daddy?"

"Don't tell your brother or sister about the monsters... we don't want them to get scared..."

"Okay Daddy..." Jay said as we closed the door and went over to Keisha and Troy's house.

"Mommy! Daddy!" they squealed when Keisha let us in...

"Did you get in trouble?" Amina asked...

"Nope..." Jay beamed...

"I got in trouble..." Amina sighed...

"You did?"

"Yea – but I got a good report this time – right Mommy?"

"Yes Amina..." Keisha answered...

"We're gonna visit with Auntie Keisha – y'all go play..." I said...

"Okay!" they squealed in unison and then they ran upstairs as Troy came in...

"Sup y'all – where's my Mina – Mina!"

"Troy – let 'em stay upstairs..." Keisha said...

"Oh shit – what's wrong? Y'all good?"

"I don't even know where to start..." I answered as tears streamed down my face...

"Beautiee... please... don't cry..." Bazil said as he wiped my tears and then he started tearing up...

"My baby is so brave... but he's scared..."

"Wai' a min – what the fuck happened?" Keisha asked...

"Come sit down..." Bazil sighed. After we all sat down Bazil spoke... "When's the last time you've been in your backyard?"

"Why? What the fuck is going on?" Troy snapped...

"Troy!" Keisha snapped...

"I'm sorry..." Troy said...

"That's okay – when's the last time you've been in your backyard?" Bazil asked again...

"Bazil – what the fuck is going on?" Troy asked...

"Jay drew this picture..." Bazil sighed as he put the picture on the table...

"Oh shit! He caught y'all fuckin!" Keisha laughed...

"Look at this..." Bazil said as he pointed to the stick figures in the grass...

"Yo... what the fuck!" Troy exclaimed...

"Jay told his teacher this was Mommy and Daddy... and this is the monsters..."

"Monsters?" Keisha asked...

"Jay said the monsters play in the backyard at night..." I sighed...

10

"Wait... this is why you asked me about our backyard?" Troy asked...

"Yea..."

"Bazil... I don't mean any harm..."

"You think I'm crazy..." Bazil sighed...

"I know you ain't crazy – Beautiee was cryin' – Jay was scared – something happened in that backyard..." Keisha said...

"I asked Jay to show me where the monsters were... he pointed outside... he was so scared he was shaking... he didn't want me to go in the backyard but I had to..."

"Oh shit! Somebody was in your backyard?" Troy asked...

"Yea..."

"Damn Bazil – I'm sorry..."

"That's okay – but we need to check your backyard..." Bazil said as he got up and we all went towards the backyard... "Stay here..." Bazil said as he and Troy went outside. Keisha and I watched them intently and we knew what was happening as soon as their expression changed...

"Oh shit – something happened in our backyard?" Keisha asked even though she already knew the answer...

"We gotta keep this door locked..." Troy answered...

"Fuck this – I'm calling the police..." Keisha said as she picked up her cell phone...

"Keisha – wait!" Bazil snapped...

"Fuck that – I ain't waitin' for shit!"

"Keisha... wait... please..." I said as I touched her hand...

"Aiight..." she said as she put her cell phone down... "What the fuck am I waiting for?"

"Jay told me the monsters make noise when they play..." Bazil said...

"Oh hell no!" Keisha said as she went to pick up her phone but Troy snatched it before she could...

"Keisha – listen!" Troy exclaimed...

"I'm listening!" Keisha snapped...

"I told Jay to wake me up tonight when the monsters are in the backyard... and when he does... I'ma handle them my damn self..." Bazil said...

"That's what I'm talkin' about!" Troy exclaimed... "You want me to help you handle 'em?"

"Fuck that – you need to stay here and handle the monsters in our yard!" Keisha snapped...

"Keisha's right..." Bazil agreed...

"Amina! Come downstairs!" Troy yelled...

"Troy – leave her alone!" Keisha snapped...

"Yes Daddy?" Amina said as they all came into the kitchen...

"There's Daddy's girl..." he said as he picked her up...

"I love you Daddy..."

"I love you too..." Troy said as he hugged her tight...

"Daddy... I can't breathe..."

"Sorry..." Troy laughed as he put her down...

"Can we go finish playing?" Amina asked...

"Amina... we need to go home..." I answered...

"Aww man!"

"They comin' back tomorrow Amina – you act like you ain't gonna see them again..." Keisha laughed...

"Can they spend the night?"

"Amina – you know this is a school night – right?" I asked...

"Yea..." she sighed...

"You can spend the night this weekend – if it's okay with Mom and Dad..."

"It's okay – right Mommy?"

"Hell yea – what time you need me to bring her over?" Keisha laughed...

"We'll let you know later..." Bazil answered...

"C'mon kids – let's go..." Bazil said as he went towards the door and the kids followed...

"Bazil..." Troy called out...

"I'll call you – Beautice – let's go..." When we got inside Bazil didn't say anything...

"Mommy?"

"Yes Joy?"

"Did you and Daddy have a fight?"

"No baby... we didn't have a fight..."

"Can I go on your computer?"

"Joy – you already know the library is off limits..." Bazil answered...

"But Daddy..." I could see Bazil was about to explode so I stopped him...

"Joy – go upstairs with your brothers – Joseph – show your sister how to turn on the netbook..."

"Okay Mommy – c'mon Joy..." he said as he took her hand and they went upstairs..."

"Daddy?"

"Yes Jay..."

"Are you okay?"

"Daddy's okay – I got my big boy making sure I'm okay..." Bazil answered as he picked Jay up and hugged him...

"I love you Daddy..."

"I love you too... but right now I need to talk to Mommy..."

"Okay Daddy – I'll go upstairs..." Bazil put him down and he ran upstairs to play...

"Bazil – talk to me..." Bazil didn't say anything – he just pulled me into a hug and we held each other... "I'm scared..."

"Me too..."

"What are we gonna do?"

"I'm going to make lasagna for dinner..."

"Oh my... the kids will sleep good tonight..."

"Yes they will..." he breathed as he pulled me into a kiss...

"They might go to sleep early..."

"They might..."

"We'll have plenty of time for dessert..."

"Indeed..."

14

"I love you..."

"I love you too..."

"Me too!" Joy squealed as she came running into the kitchen...

"What are you doing in here?" I laughed as I picked her up...

"What's for dinner?"

"Go back upstairs Joy..." I answered as I put her down...

"But I'm hungry..." she whined...

"Little girl – if you don't take your ass back upstairs!" I laughed...

"Okay Mommy!" she said as she hurried back upstairs...

"She's not stupid..." Bazil laughed...

"She's not like her brothers – that's for sure..."

"They know when something's going on – they just handle it different..."

"I know..."

"I sure hope we can go back to normal after tonight..."

"So do I..." I sighed...

"Poor Jay – you know – it's crazy that my son is helping me in this situation – we're the parents – it's our job to protect them..."

"He was so scared earlier – but he's happy to help his Daddy – where you like that when you were little?"

"Yea... I was..." Bazil sighed as he turned his head away...

"Bazil – come here..." I said as I pulled him into a hug and he started crying...

"I wish they were still alive – Jay is just like my father..."

"I'm sure they know..."

"You think so?"

"Of course – I bet you're just like your father too..."

"Really?"

"Let's just say I'm sure your mother was very happy..."

"She was..." Bazil said as he smiled at me mischievously. I sat there and watched as Bazil took all the ingredients out of the refrigerator and the cabinets and then he started making the lasagna...

"Mommy?"

"Yes Joy..." I sighed...

"I wanna stay down here..."

"Why?"

"I just don't wanna play upstairs..."

"Jay! Joseph!"

"Yes Mommy?" they answered in unison...

"Come downstairs!"

"Okay!" they answered again as they came running downstairs and into the kitchen...

"Go sit at the table with your sister..."

"Okay!" they squealed as they hurried over to the table and sat down...

"Where are you going Mommy?" Joy asked...

16

"I'll be right back..." I answered as I walked out the kitchen and went into the library. I went in my desk drawer, pulled out coloring books, and crayons, and went back into the kitchen...

"Ooohhh... we're gonna color?" Joseph squealed...

"We're gonna color..." I answered as I sat down at the table with them... "As soon as Daddy puts the food in the oven – and Daddy's gonna color too..."

"Yeaaa!" they squealed as Bazil looked at me...

"I'll" be over there in a few minutes..." Bazil said as he got the aluminum foil out the cabinet, put some over the lasagna, put it in the oven, and then came over to the table...

"Joy – pick out a coloring book and crayons..." I said...

"Okay – I want this one!" she squealed as she picked up a coloring book and a box of crayons..."Okay Joseph – pick out a coloring book and crayons...

"Okay Mommy..."

"Okay Jay – your turn!"

"Okay Mommy..."

"Okay Daddy – your turn!" I laughed...

"Okay Mommy!" Bazil laughed along with the kids...

"Okay – I get this one – everybody color a picture in their book – and if you finish your picture before dinner is ready – color another

17

one..." I explained as we all started coloring. It took about 45 minutes for the lasagna to cook so we finished all the pictures in our coloring books right before the timer went off... "Okay – give me your coloring books and crayons – Jay – help Mommy set the table..."

"Okay Mommy!" Jay exclaimed as he got up and went to get the silverware and the napkins, and proceeded to set the table. I took the coloring books and crayons back into the library and when I came back into the kitchen Bazil was already putting the plates of lasagna on the table...

"That looks good..." I said as I sat down...

"Okay – everyone hold hands..." Bazil said as we all grabbed hands...

"I'll say grace!" Joy exclaimed...

"Okay Joy – go ahead..." Bazil said...

"God – thank you for my family, thank you for this food, and thank you for telling Mommy to buy coloring books – amen!"

"Amen! We all said in unison and then we started eating...

"Mommy?"

"Yes Joy..."

"Did you color with grandma and grandpa when you were little?"

"Yes... I did..."

"Did you like it?"

"Yes I did..."

"Joy – let Mommy eat..." Bazil said...

"Did you like coloring Daddy?" Jay asked...

"Yes Jay – now let's finish eating – it's almost time for bed..." We didn't say anything else – all you could hear was clanging of forks on plates until we were finished...

"Okay – Jay – help Daddy put the dishes in the dishwasher and then we'll have something to drink..."

"Can we have some ice cream?"

"No Jay – we're going to have something to drink – and then we're going upstairs – okay?" Bazil said...

"Okay Daddy..." Jay said and then they put the dishes in the dishwasher... "Okay – we have cherry, grape, or orange..."

"Orange!" they all said in unison...

"Okay! Orange Hi-C coming right up!" Bazil boomed as the kids laughed. The kids sat at the table and waited as Bazil put 3 cups on the table and poured the Hi-C...

"Thank you Daddy!" they said in unison. After they finished their juice they put their cups in the dishwasher, Bazil put the food away, and the kids ran upstairs...

"Mrs. Osgood?"

"Yes Mr. Osgood?"

"What would you like to drink?"

"I'd like Henney... on ice..."

"Coming right up..." he said, smiling mischievously...

"We're gonna have to start locking our door..."

"I know..." Bazil laughed as he handed me my drink and we went into the living room... "Come sit down here..." Bazil said as he sat down on the couch and patted for me to go sit next to him...

"Okay..."

"Here..." he said as he picked up my drink and handed it to me...

"Thank you..." I said as I took it from him and then I gulped it down...

"Thirsty huh?" he laughed...

"Kinda..." I laughed as I lay back against him and he held me. Bazil finished his drink and just as we were getting comfortable Joy called us...

"Mommy! Daddy!"

"So much for that..." Bazil laughed as we got up and went upstairs...

"Yes Joy?" I answered as we went into her room...

"Can I stay up late? Please?"

"What time is it?"

"Ummm..."

"What time is it?"

"7:30..."

"What time do you go to bed?"

"8:00... but..."

"You can go to bed now... or you can go to bed at 8:00 – which one do you want?"

"I wanna go to bed now – and watch tv until 8:00!" she squealed...

"Okay – that's fine..." I said as she got in the bed and turned on the tv...

"Good night Mommy, good night Daddy... I love you..."

"We love you too..." Bazil said as he kissed her good night, I kissed her goodnight, and then we went to the boys' room...

"Hi Mommy! Hi Daddy! We playin'!" Jay laughed...

"I see..." Bazil laughed...

"We're going to go lay down – you know what time you go to bed – right?" I asked...

"Yes Mommy!" they answered in unison and then they went back to playing...

"Come with me..." Bazil said as he took me by the hand and pulled me out the room...

"Bazil..."

"Hurry up..." Bazil whispered as he pulled me into the room, closed the door, locked it, and pushed me down onto the bed...

"Bazil... we can't..."

"Yes..." he breathed as he climbed on top of me, opened his pants, took out his dick, and thrust himself inside me... "We can..."

"Bazil..." I moaned...

"Yes Beautiee..." he breathed in my ear...

"Daddy! Daddy!"

"I'm coming Jay!" Bazil said as he jumped up off me, unlocked the door, and snatched the door open...

"The monsters..."

"Show me..." Bazil said as they took off running down the hall into the boys' room with me following behind them...

"Right there!" Jay whispered as he pointed at his window...

"Mi Lydia ... te necesito por favor ... Mi Lidia... I need you... please..."

"Bazil ... yo también te necesito ... Bazil... I need you too..." she breathed as she clung to him...

"Mi Lydia ... te sientes tan bien ... todavía te sientes bien ... incluso en la muerte ... Mi

Lydia... you feel so good... you still feel good... even in death..." he breathed as he laid her down in the grass...

"Sí Bazil ... hazme el amor ... te anhelo ... Yes Bazil... make love to me... I crave you..."

"No entiendo... I don't understand..." he breathed as he kissed her... "Estoy muerto ... pero todavía muy vivo ... I'm dead... but still very much alive..." he breathed as he took his dick out his pants...

"Sí Bazil ... te quiero ... soy tuyo en la vida ... y en la muerte ... hazme el amor ... por favor ... Yes Bazil... I want you... I'm yours in life... and in death... make love to me... please..."

"Si mi Lydia ... Yes Mi Lydia..." Bazil breathed as he eased himself inside her...

"Oh Bazil ... Sí ... Eso es ... No te detengas ... Oh Bazil... Yes... That's it... Don't stop..."

"Mi Lydia ... tu coño se siente como la noche en que hicimos el amor por primera vez ... Mi Lydia... your pussy feels just like the night we made love for the first time..." he said as he started thrusting...

"Bazil ... ¿cómo es esto posible? Bazil... how is this possible?"

"No me importa... I don't care..." he breathed as he kissed her hard and fucked her deeper...

"Huh... Huh... Huh... Huh..."

"Uuugh! Uuugh! Uuugh! Uuugh!"

"Bazil ... me estoy acabando... Bazil... I'm cumming..."

23

"Cum para mi ... Cum for me..."

"Haah...   Haah...   Haah...   Haah... HAAAAAH!"

"Uuugh!   Uuugh!   Uuugh!   Uuugh! UUUUUGGGHHHH!"

"Te quiero mucho... I love you so much..." Lydia said as she started crying...

"Mi Lydia..." he breathed as he kissed her eyes... "Por favor ... no llores ... Please... don't cry..."

"No puedo evitarlo ... me temo ... I can't help it... I'm afraid..."

"Yo te protegere... I'll protect you..."

"Nuestro nieto está en la ventana ... Our grandson is in the window..."

"Lo sé... I know..."

"¿Por qué no le dirá a su padre? Why won't he tell his father?"

"Es un niño ... tiene miedo ... He's a child... he's afraid..."

"¿Qué pasa si Bazil nunca viene? What if Bazil never comes?"

"Bazil vendrá ... lo prometo ... Bazil will come... I promise..."

"Quiero confiar en ti... I want to trust you..."

"¿Te he decepcionado alguna vez? Have I ever let you down?"

"No pero... No... but..."

"Mi Lydia..." he breathed and then he kissed her again... "Te amo ... por favor ... confía en mí ... I love you... please... trust me..."

"Te amo ... por favor ... confía en mí ... I love you... I want to be with you always..."

"Vas a... You will..."

"Deseo que la Corporación de Paisajismo nunca haya creado ese fertilizante ... I wish the Landscaping Corporation never created that fertilizer..."

"¿No me siento bien contigo? Don't I feel good to you?"

"Sí Bazil ... te sientes bien conmigo ... pero me siento Clayton ... y él no se siente bien ... y estoy asustada ... Yes Bazil... you feel good to me... but I feel Clayton... and he doesn't feel good... and I'm scared..." she said as she started crying again...

"No Mi Lydia... Por favor... please..." Bazil breathed as he kissed her... "Sienteme... Feel me..." he breathed as he eased himself inside her again...

"Bazil ... Sí ... te siento ... Bazil... Yes... I feel you..." she moaned as he covered her mouth with his, put his tongue in her mouth, tongued her down, and fucked her harder and deeper...

"Mmmm! Mmmm! Mmmm! Mmmm!"

"Mmmph! Mmmph! Mmmph! Mmmph!"

"Mmmm! Mmmm! Mmmm! Mmmm! MMMMMMMM!"

"Mmmph! Mmmph! Mmmph! Mmmph! MMMMMMMPPPHHHH!"

"Come here Jay..." I said as I picked him up, we went to look out the window... and I wasn't prepared for what I saw... "What the fuck?" I whispered...

"They're playing – like you and Daddy..." Jay whispered. I continued looking out the window as the zombies were literally fucking in our backyard...

"Mmmm! Mmmm! Mmmm! Mmmm!"
"Mmmph! Mmmph! Mmmph! Mmmph!"
"Bazil ... para ... Bazil... stop..."
"Mi Lydia ... por favor ... te sientes tan bien ... no me hagas parar ... Mi Lydia... please... you feel so good... don't make me stop..." he breathed as he pulled out of her, lifted her dress, and began kissing her down her body...

"Bazil ... oh si ... Bazil... oh yes..." she moaned. He continued kissing his way down, spread her legs, and dove in...

"BAAAZZZIIILLLL!" she moaned as she grabbed his head with her hands and locked her legs around his head... "Aaah... Aaah... Aaah..." she was coming in his mouth, her nectar was sweet, and he was thirsty... "AAAAAAGGGHHHH!" he continued licking, sucking, and slurping until she spoke... "Bazil ... él viene ... Bazil... he's coming..."

"No, Mi Lydia ... te protegeré ... No Mi Lydia... I'll protect you..."

"I'm going downstairs Beautiee – stay here with the boys..." Bazil whispered as he went into the boys' closet, grabbed the wooden bat, ran downstairs into the kitchen, and out into the backyard...

"Bazil ... nuestro hijo está aquí ... Bazil... our son is here..."

"Oh, mierda! Oh shit!" Bazil exclaimed as he jumped up off Lydia, helped her up, and they fixed their clothes and waited for their son to come into the backyard. I continued to look out the window and I was shocked to see the zombies get up off the ground and start a conversation...

"What the fuck are they doing?"

"They're talking to Daddy..." Jay whispered...

"Hello Bazil..." his father said...

"What the fuck – am I high?!" Bazil exclaimed...

"What the hell took you so long?" Lydia asked...

"Mom? Dad?"

"Yes Son..." his father answered...

"What are you doing here?" Bazil asked...

"We need your help..." his mother answered...

"Mom... Dad... how..."

"Bazil – we don't have a lot of time..." his mother said...

"Mom... please..." Bazil said as he started crying...

"Bazil..."

"Yes Dad?"

"We need your help..."

"You're DEAD!" Bazil snapped... "I'm ALIVE! My son is scared to death! Why are you here?"

"BAZIL!" his father boomed...

"Yes Dad..."

"We didn't mean to scare Jay..."

"How the fuck do you know his name?"

"Bazil... he's our grandchild..." his mother said...

"Your grandchild thinks you're monsters!"

"Bazil – we tried to get your attention – but he saw us... and you didn't..." his mother said...

"You wanted to get my attention by fucking in my backyard?"

"Bazil – we're running out of time – you're running out of time..." his father said...

"Running out of time – wait a minute – am I dying?"

"No son – you're not dying... not yet..."

"What the fuck is that supposed to mean?"

"They're coming..." his mother answered...

"Who's coming?"

"Zombies..."

"Troy – stop playin'!" Bazil laughed...

"Troy's not here..." his father said...

"Stop... I can't..." Bazil laughed...

"GOT DAMMIT BAZIL WILL YOU LISTEN!" his father boomed...

"Sure... I'll play along... I'll listen... tell me all about the zombies..." he laughed...

"The Landscaping Corporation developed a new fertilizer..." his mother explained...

"What does fertilizer have to do with zombies?" Bazil laughed...

"When people use this new fertilizer... it gets absorbed into the ground – once you water it – you trigger something in the fertilizer that wakes us up... and..." his father explained...

"And what?"

"We wind up in backyards... or graveyards... or parks... fucking through eternity..." his father sighed...

"Wait a minute – you're telling me that this fertilizer wakes up the dead – and makes you fuck?"

"It doesn't make us fuck – but we're dead – we can't control our urges..."

"My son drew a picture for his teacher..." Bazil started to explain..."

"I know... I'm sorry..." his father said...

"You're sorry? What the fuck am I supposed to do? What if they school sends an investigator to our house because they suspect we're abusing him?"

"Bazil – you need to tell them to stop using the fertilizer... before it's too late..."

"Sure Dad – I'll just call the Landscaping Corporation – I'll tell them I had a conversation with my dead parents – who told me about the fertilizer – and when they ask me if I was hallucinating I'll tell them I have proof – because my son caught them fucking in my backyard!"

"Mommy... the monsters made Daddy mad..." Jay whispered as we continued watching...

"Bazil... please... help us... help all of us..." his mother pleaded...

"I CAN'T!" Bazil yelled...

"Son... please... you have to do this..."

"And you have to get the fuck outta my backyard!" Bazil yelled as he swung the bat and his father caught it and snatched it from him...

"No... Daddy!" Jay cried...

"Jay – be quiet – you'll wake up your brother and sister..." I said...

"BAZIL – LISTEN!" his father boomed...

"Yes Dad?"

"They'll be others... once they see the others... they'll believe you..."

"Others?"

"We have to go now... we love you... kiss our grandchildren..." his mother said as they both went back into the hole in the grass and disappeared...

"Yeaa!" Jay squealed...

"Be quiet!" I snapped...

"Mommy?" Joseph said as he sat up, rubbing his eyes...

"Go back to sleep Joseph... everything's okay..." I whispered...

"I'm sorry Mommy..." Jay said with tears in his eyes...

"That's okay – you did a good job helping Daddy..."

"I did?"

"Yes Jay – now go to sleep..." I said as I put him in the bed and pulled up the covers...

"I love you Mommy..."

"I love you too..."

"Me too Mommy?" Joseph asked...

"Yes Joseph – you too..." I whispered as I closed their door and went downstairs...

CHAPTER 5

"Beautiee..." Bazil breathed when he saw me. I didn't bother asking if he was okay because I knew he wasn't... "I need to tell you something..."

"I know..."

"Beautiee... you don't understand..."

"I know that too..."

"That doesn't make any sense..." he laughed...

"I know that too..." I laughed...

"I love you..."

"I know that too..." I said and then I went over to the counter, took two glasses out the cabinet, put in some ice, and poured us drinks...

"You're not going to believe it..."

"Try me..." I said as we sat down at the table. Bazil sighed before he began...

"The zombies... are my parents..."

"Your parents? That explains it..." I said as I sipped my drink...

"Explains it? What are you talking about?"

"Jay and I were watching you – we saw you talking – we saw you get angry – Jay said the monsters made Daddy mad..."

"Beautiee! Why would you let him watch what was happening?!"

"Really? You're really asking me why I let your son watch you argue with zombies?"

"I need another drink..." he laughed as he got up...

"Bring the bottle..." I laughed. Bazil brought the bottle to the table and then he continued...

"My parents told me they need my help..."

"Help with what? They're dead!"

"That's what I said..."

"Jay cried when he saw you try to hit the zombie..."

"That was my father..." he said as he poured us another drink...

"Bazil – what did they say?"

"They said they need my help..."

"Help with what?"

"I can't believe I'm saying this..."

"Bazil... please..."

"They said they've been trying to get my attention... but Jay saw them first..."

"Wait a minute – they've been trying to get your attention – by fucking in the backyard?"

"That's exactly what I asked them..."

"What do they need your help with?" Bazil picked up his glass, finished his drink, poured himself another one, took a sip, and took a deep breath before he continued...

"The Landscaping Corporation created a new fertilizer..." he sighed...

"What does fertilizer have to do with zombies?"

"Finish your drink..."

"Okay..." I sighed as I picked up my glass and took a sip...

"The fertilizer by itself is fine – but once you water it... it gets absorbed into the soil... wakes up the dead... and..."

"What Bazil?"

"They can't stop fucking..." he sighed...

"Wait..." I laughed... "Your parents have been fucking in our backyard..." I laughed again... "Because people have been using fertilizer?"

"Yes Beautiee..."

"People are going to think we're crazy..."

"That's what I said... but..."

"But what?"

"My father said we're running out of time..."

"Oh my God – you're dying?"

"No Beautiee – I'm not dying – the zombies are coming..."

"What?"

"My father said they're coming..."

"The Zombies?"

"Yes..."

35

"How the hell are you supposed to stop the zombies?"

"My father wants me to tell the Landscaping Corporation to stop producing the fertilizer so people will stop using it..."

"Oh that's great – you just tell them your dead parents were fucking in your backyard to get your attention so you could tell them about their fertilizer..."

"My father said I won't have to worry about them thinking I'm crazy because they'll be more..."

"More? Shit – I need another drink..."

"We finished the bottle..."

"What... how..."

"C'mon – let's go to bed..." he said as he got up from the table and extended his hand for me to take...

"Okay..." I sighed as I took his hand and got up...

"Come with me..." he said as he pulled me out the kitchen towards the stairs...

"Bazil... wait..." I laughed as he pulled me up the stairs. When we got to the top of the stairs, he pulled me into the bedroom, closed the door, locked it, and pushed me down onto the bed... "Bazil... we can't..."

"Yes..." he said as he climbed on top of me, loosened his pants, took out his dick, and thrust himself inside me... "We can..."

"Bazil..." I moaned...

"Yes... Beautiee..." he breathed in my ear as I grabbed his ass, wrapped my legs around him, and pulled him in deeper.

CHAPTER 6

"Don't stop..." I moaned...

"I won't..." Bazil breathed...

"Bazil... I'm cumming..."

"Mommy! Daddy!"

"Fuck... I'm cumming... Uuuggghhh!"

"Mommy! Daddy! I'm ready for school!" Joy squealed outside our bedroom door...

"I'll be there in a minute..." I sighed...

"Whatcha doin' Mommy?" she asked as Bazil laughed while kissing me...

"I'm... in... the... bathroom..."

"Okay Mommy – hurry up!" she said and then she skipped down the hall...

"I don't wanna get up..." I breathed as we continued kissing...

"Neither do I..."

"I better get up... she'll be back..." I laughed...

"Good thing we locked the door..." Bazil laughed as he got up off me...

"I'm going to the bathroom... while I have a chance..." I laughed...

"I'm coming with you..." Bazil said as he followed me into the bathroom, pushed me back against the sink, lifted my leg up... and slid inside me...

"Bazil... the kids..."

"You want me to stop?"

"No..." I moaned as I wrapped my arms around his neck...

"I didn't think so..." he breathed and then he grabbed my ass and thrust his tongue in my mouth...

"Mommy! You still in the bathroom?"

"I'll be right there Joy..." I yelled as I pushed Bazil away from me and he began to pout... "I'll make it up to you – I promise..." I whispered as I hurried to open the bedroom door... "Oh my goodness – you look pretty – did you pick that out?" I asked as Bazil came out behind me, tying his robe around him...

"Uh huh..."

"You look like a princess..." Bazil said...

"Thank you Daddy!" she beamed...

"Go downstairs – we're gonna check on your brothers..." Bazil said as we went down the hall to the boys' room...

"Good morning Mommy, good morning Daddy – we ready!" Joseph beamed...

"You look good – go downstairs with your sister – we need to talk to Jay..." Bazil said...

"Okay Daddy..." Joseph said as he skipped out the room...

"Am I in trouble?" Jay asked...

"No Jay – Daddy's very proud of you..."

"You are?"

"Yes Jay – but I still need your help..."

"Okay Daddy..."

"We're gonna make the monsters go away – but I don't want you to tell your brother or you sister – we don't want to scare them..."

"Okay Daddy – I won't tell them..."

"Don't tell your teacher either..." I said...

"Why Mommy?"

"What did your mother say?"

"Yes Daddy..."

"Good – c'mon – let's get your breakfast before your bus comes..." Bazil said as he took Jay by the hand and we went downstairs to the kitchen...

"Here Jay..." Joseph said as he handed Jay a pop tart... "I got one for you..."

"Thank you Joseph..." Jay said as he opened the pop tart and started eating...

"Who is it?" I asked...

"It's Mina!" she squealed...

"Coming Mina!" Joy squealed as she ran to the door...

"Daddy – can you help me open the door?"

"Yes Joy..." Bazil laughed as he opened the door..."

"Good morning Uncle Bazil, good morning Auntie Beautiee..." Amina said as she ran over to the kids...

"Good morning y'all..." Keisha said as she came in...

"Good morning..." we both said in unison...

"C'mon y'all – your bus is here..." Keisha said as Troy came in...

"Bye!" they all said in unison as they ran out the door and we watched them get on the bus. Once they got on the bus, Keisha went right in...

"Aiight – I waited – we callin' the police – right?"

"C'mon – I'll put on a pot of coffee..." Bazil sighed...

"Bazil – I'm not havin' this shit..." Keisha said...

"Keisha – hold on – you know Bazil ain't havin' it either..."

"Keisha – please – come have some coffee..." I sighed...

"You lucky I love y'all..." she said as she went in the kitchen and sat down. Troy sat down beside her and nobody said anything as Bazil made the coffee. When it was done, he took 4 mugs out the cabinet, poured the coffee, added the sugar, added the hazelnut creamer, picked up two of the mugs, and brought them to the table. I picked up the other mugs, brought them to the table, and we both sat down with them...

"Last night, we put the kids to bed, and then we went to lie down..." Bazil said...

41

"Okay..." Keisha said...

"As soon as we lay down, Jay came to get me..."

"Oh shit!" Troy exclaimed...

"I told him to show me, we ran to his room, and I looked out the window..."

"Oh shit!" Keisha exclaimed...

"I took Jay's baseball bat out the closet, went downstairs, and went in the backyard... and..." Bazil couldn't finish... he got choked up...

"Bazil saw his parents..." I said...

"I thought your parents were dead?" Troy asked...

"They are..." I answered...

"Wai' a min – the monsters are your parents?" Keisha asked...

"Yes..." Bazil answered...

"So... your dead parents..." Troy started to say...

"Have been fucking in my backyard – scaring the shit out of my son..." Bazil sighed as he finished his coffee...

"Why?" Keisha asked...

"They need my help..."

"They need your help? They're dead!" Keisha exclaimed...

"That's what I said..." Bazil said...

"What do they need your help with?" Troy asked...

"They want me to tell the Landscaping Corporation to stop producing their new fertilizer..." Bazil sighed...

"They're dead! What the fuck?" Troy exclaimed...

"I know..."

"Why do they want you to tell them to stop producing the fertilizer?" Keisha asked...

"Because... when you water your flowers... there's an ingredient in the fertilizer that gets absorbed into the soil... and..."

"Oh Hell No!" Troy exclaimed...

"Yea..." Bazil sighed...

"The fertilizer wakes up the dead... and makes them fuck?" Keisha asked...

"The way my parents explained it – it doesn't make them fuck – but they can't control their urges..." Bazil sighed...

"That's not all they said..." I sighed...

"How you know?" Keisha asked...

"I told her..." Bazil answered...

"You didn't think he was crazy?"

"We watched him have a conversation with the zombies – I mean his parents... we watched them get mad... Bazil tried to hit them with the bat... is father snatched it..."

"What the fuck?!" Troy exclaimed...

"Scared the shit outta me too..." Bazil laughed...

"He didn't try to hit you with it?" Keisha asked...

"No... but..."

"He told Bazil they're coming..." I sighed...

"Who's coming?" Troy asked...

"Zombies..." Bazil answered...

43

"Your parents came to warn you..." Keisha said...

"Exactly..." Bazil said...

"Aiight – so what we doin?"

"We're going to the police..." Bazil answered.

"Stop... I can't!" Chandler laughed as he was holding his stomach...

"I'M NOT CRAZY!" she screamed as we walked in...

"Mr. Osgood! How are ya?" one of the officers greeted...

"Good morning – we need to speak with Chandler..." Bazil said...

"Lady – get outta here before I call somebody and have you committed..." Chandler laughed...

"Ms. Shelby?"

"Mr. Osgood – thank God you're here – tell them – I'm not crazy – your son saw them too – tell them!"

"Dad? What's she talking about?" Chandler asked...

"Dad? Oh my God – Sergeant Corbett is your son?" Ms. Shelby asked...

"Y'all come inside..." Chandler said as we all walked into Chandler's office and he closed the door...

"What are you doing?" one of the officers whispered...

"The fuck you think I'm doing? SHHH!" the officer answered as he crept up to the door...

"Hold on..." Chandler said as he looked at the door and saw the officer's shadow... "I SEE YOU!" Chandler yelled...

"Uh huh – that's what your ass get!" one of the officer's yelled as they all laughed when the officer stepped away from Chandler's door and went back behind the desk...

"Okay – what's going on?" Chandler asked...

"Ms. Shelby – these are my friends, Mr. & Mrs. Cochran..." Bazil said...

"Mr. & Mrs. Cochran – are you Amina's parents?"

"Yes we are..." Troy beamed...

"It's nice to meet you – your daughter is in the class across from me – she comes to my class every day to see Jay and Charles – she's a little darling..."

"Thank you..." Keisha said...

"Ms. Shelby is Jay's teacher..." Bazil said as he sat down... "She called us in for a conference because Jay drew a picture and told her it was a picture of us and it was also a picture of monsters in the backyard..."

"So... Ms. Shelby just told me that she saw zombies fuckin' in her backyard – is that what my brother saw?" Chandler asked...

"Yea..." Bazil sighed... "And they've been in their backyard too..." he said as he nodded towards Keisha and Troy...

"Oh my God! What are we going to do?!" Ms. Shelby shrieked...

"Ms. Shelby – if you don't mind – I need to speak to my son-in-law..." Bazil said...

"Hell yea I mind!! What about me?!" she snapped...

"I'll keep in touch with you..." Chandler said...

"You'll keep in touch? What the hell does that even mean?"

"Ms. Shelby – I took your report – I know you're not crazy – I'll get back to you..."

"Mr. Osgood – you'll tell me what's going on – right?"

"My son-in-law will keep you up-to-date..."

"What about your son? We can bring him in here and..."

"Ms. Shelby?"

"Yes Mr. Osgood?"

"Leave my son out of it..." Bazil said as he got up to open the door...

"Fine!" she snapped as she got up and stormed out. Bazil closed the door and came to sit back down beside me and then he continued...

"I can't discuss this with her..."

"Dad – I don't understand..."

"Chandler – I'm going to explain it – but I need you to listen to me..."

"Okay..."

"After we met with Ms. Shelby, I brought the picture home. I showed it to Keisha and Troy, and we went in their backyard..."

"Did you see zombies?" Chandler asked...

"No – they only come out when it's dark..."

"This some bullshit..."

"Chandler... listen..." Bazil said...

"Okay..."

"When we went in the backyard, we could tell something happened back there..."

"It was dug up..." Troy said...

"Dug up like what? Like a grave?" Chandler asked...

"It was more like something came up out the dirt..." Troy answered...

"You didn't tell me that Troy!" Keisha snapped...

"I know... I'm sorry..."

"We locked the door, and then we took the kids home..." Bazil said...

"When did you see the zombies?" Chandler asked...

"We had dinner, we went to bed, and Jay saw the monsters in the backyard, so I took the

48

bat out of the closet, I went downstairs, I went in the backyard... and that's when I found out the monsters were actually my parents..."

"Y'all been drinking?" Chandler asked...

"Hell yea!" I laughed...

"I'm serious!" Chandler snapped...

"So are we..." we all said in unison...

"My parents have been coming in my backyard to tell me they need my help... and to warn me..."

"They're DEAD!" Chandler snapped...

"I swear to God – if one more person tells me my parents are dead..." Bazil sighed as he put his head in his hands...

"I'm sorry Dad... go 'head..."

"They need me to contact the Landscaping Corporation and tell them to stop producing their new fertilizer..."

"Why?"

"Because when you water your plants, there's an ingredient in the fertilizer that gets absorbed into the soil... and it wakes them up... and..."

"They start fuckin?" Chandler asked...

"Yea..."

"Aaaaahaaaaa! Aaaaahaaaaa!"

"This isn't funny Chandler..."

"I know..." he laughed... "I'm sorry... but..."

"Maybe they should sell it as a treatment for impotence – if it wakes up the dead – imagine what it can do for you?" Troy laughed...

"Damn Troy..." Keisha laughed... "That's fucked up... sorry y'all..."

"Actually... that's funny..." Bazil laughed...

"They're gonna think we're smoking some good shit..." I laughed...

"I wish we were..." Bazil sighed...

"Me too..." Chandler said... "Dad?"

"Yes Chandler?"

"What was the warning?"

"They're coming..."

"Oh shit!"

"Yea..."

"We have to contact the news..."

"I know..."

"Sarge – you're not going to believe this!" the officer said as he snatched the door open...

"What's wrong?"

"We just got another call about zombies in the backyard!"

"Shit!" Chandler said as he got up and went out to take the report...

CHAPTER 8

"Mr. Osgood, Mrs. Osgood – nice to see you – is everything alright?" the substitute teacher asked...

"Everything's fine – I'm here to pick up my sons, my daughter, Charles, and Amina..." Bazil answered...

"Are you sure everything's okay?" she asked...

"Everything's fine – we have a surprise for them..." Bazil answered...

"Oh that's nice – have you been to the main office?"

"Yes Maam..."

"I'm sorry – normally I wouldn't ask – but since you're getting Charles and Amina – you know Amina's across the hall – right?"

"Yes – her parents are there..."

"Okay – that's fine – I'll go get Jay and Charles..." she said as she went into the class room...

"Thank God she isn't asking too many questions..." I laughed...

"Daddy! Uncle Bazil! Uncle Troy!" they squealed when they saw us...

"Hello boys..." Bazil said...

"We thought we was goin' to the principal's office..." Charles laughed...

"Amina!" Jay Squealed...

"Jay! Charles! Mommy – where we goin'?"

"C'mon y'all..." Keisha said as we all hurried out the school before anyone could stop us...

"Daddy – we goin' on vacation?" Amina asked...

"It's a surprise..." Troy answered as they all got in the car...

"Where we goin' Uncle Bazil?" Charles asked...

"It's a surprise..." I answered as we all got in the car and headed for Chandler's house...

"Grandpa! Grandma!" Chelsea, Kalliyah, and Chandler Jr. said as Starr opened the door...

"Hi Daddy, hi Beautiee – what are you doing here?" Bazil pulled her into a hug and held her really tight... "Daddy... are you okay?"

"I'm fine..." he breathed as he continued to hold her...

"Ummm... Daddy?"

52

"Yes Starr..."

"Are my brothers and sister here?"

"Oh – sorry about that – yes – they're coming in now..." Bazil said as Troy, Keisha, Amina, Charles, Theresa, Lil Charles, Joseph, and Jay came in...

"Yeeaaa!" the kids all squealed as they ran to each other and started hugging...

"I swear – they act like they ain't see each other in days..." Keisha laughed...

"It has been days – two to be exact – they haven't seen each other since Friday – today's Monday..." Charles laughed...

"I appreciate you picking up Charles... but what's the occasion?" Theresa asked...

"We'll talk when Chandler gets here..." Bazil sighed...

"Beautiee?" Starr whispered...

"Yes?"

"Come inside for a sec..." she whispered as we snuck outta the living room...

"Grandbabies front and center!" Bazil ordered...

"Yes sir!" they said in unison as they got in line...

"Attention!" Bazil boomed as he stood up. The grandchildren stood at attention and saluted...

"On your mark... get set... hugs!" he ordered as they ran to him and he embraced them...

"One of these days they gonna knock you over!" Troy laughed...

"Beautiee – should I be worried?" Starr whispered...

"Come here Starr..." I said as I pulled her into a hug and held her...

"I knew it..." she sighed...

"Let's go back in the living room..." I said as I started walking towards the living room and Starr followed behind me...

"Daddy!" Chelsea, Kalliyah, and Chandler Jr. squealed in unison as they ran to him...

"Y'all miss me?"

"Yes Daddy..." they all answered in unison as they hugged...

"Where's Mommy?" Chandler asked...

"I'm right here..." Starr answered as she walked up to Chandler, threw her arms around his neck, and kissed him hard...

"I love you too..." Chandler said...

"Mommy – can we spend the night?" Amina asked...

"Girl go on and play!" Keisha snapped...

"Mommy said go play!" Amina squealed as they all ran down the hall...

"Chandler? What happened?" Starr asked...

"We started getting calls this afternoon..." Chandler sighed...

"Oh shit!" Troy exclaimed...

"Chandler?"

"Starr..."

"Chandler – let me..." Bazil said...

"Daddy?"

"We had a conference with Jay's teacher..."

"Is he in trouble?"

"Starr... listen..."

"Okay..."

"Jay drew a picture of us... and a picture of monsters in the backyard..."

"Somebody was in the backyard?"

"Your grandparents..."

"I thought they were dead?"

"They are..."

"Your parents came back from the dead?" Charles asked...

"My parents have been coming in the backyard to ask for my help... and to warn me..."

"Daddy... are we in danger?"

"No... but... they need my help... and... the zombies are coming..."

"Hole up – zombies? Like Z-Nation? Like The Walking Dead?" Charles asked...

"Yea..." Chandler answered...

"Oh shit!" Charles laughed... "That was good – you almost had me..."

"He's not kidding..." Troy said...

"Oh my God – Charles..." Theresa said...

"You're not in danger Theresa – they only come out at night..."

"Oh – that's a relief!" she snapped sarcastically...

"Theresa!" Charles exclaimed...

"Charles – what do you expect me to do?"

"Theresa – we don't have a backyard..."

"We do!" Keisha snapped...

"Oh my God – I'm sorry..." Theresa sighed...

"I can't believe my grandparents came back from the dead..." Starr said...

"Ms. Shelby went to the precinct to file a report this morning..." Bazil said...

"Oh my God! Why?" Theresa exclaimed...

"Because she saw zombies in her backyard..." Chandler answered...

"Oh shit! Are you serious?" Charles exclaimed...

"I thought she was crazy too – until my father came in..." Chandler said...

"Daddy – what are you going to do?"

"I want the kids to stay here – if that's alright..."

"Of course – what about you and Beautiee?"

"We need to go back home..."

"Daddy – why can't you stay here with us? Please?"

"Starr – I can't stay here – they need me... and I need her..." he answered as he took my hand and squeezed it...

"We'll take Amina home..." Troy said...

"Let her stay here..." Bazil said...

"She'll be alright Troy..." Keisha said...

"You right – she can stay – it's okay wichall?" Troy asked...

"It's fine..." Chandler said...

"Jay!" Bazil boomed...

"Yes Daddy?" he answered as he tip-toed into the living room...

"Come with me for a minute..." Bazil said as he took Jay by the hand and they went in the guest room...

"Are you mad at me?" Jay asked...

"No Jay..."

"You promise?"

"Come here..." Bazil said as he pulled Jay into a hug and held him...

"I love you Daddy..."

"I love you too – but I need you to do something for me..."

"Okay Daddy..."

"You're gonna stay here... with Starr..."

"My brother and sister too?"

"Yes..."

"Okay Daddy..."

"Do you remember what we talked about?"

"Uh huh – I won't tell them..."

"If they hear about the monsters... tell them they don't have to be scared – okay?"

"Okay Daddy..."

"That's my big boy..." Bazil said as he pulled him into another hug..."

"Daddy?"

"Yes Jay..."

"How long do we have to stay here?"

"I don't know..." Bazil sighed...

"Am I gonna see you again?" Jay asked with tears in his eyes...

"We'll come see you every day..."

"Okay Daddy – can I go play now?"

"Yes Jay..."

"Okay!" he squealed as he ran down the hall and Bazil went back into the living room...

"What'd you tell him?" I laughed...

"I told him we'll come see him every day..." Bazil sighed...

"Amina!" Troy yelled...

"Yes Daddy?" she answered as she came running and all the kids came running behind her...

"Y'all gonna spend the night – make sure you behave..." Keisha said...

"Yeeaaa!" they all squealed as they jumped up and down, hugged, and ran back down the hall...

"I might as well cook..." Theresa sighed...

"You don't have too..." Charles said...

"Charles... we gotta eat..."

"We can go to McDonalds – we'll get happy meals for the kids – and you can relax..." he said as he took her hand...

"That's a good idea – I'll go with you..." Bazil said as he got up...

"We'll all go..." Chandler said as he got up...

"I'll be back..." Troy said as they all left...

"Starr?"

"Yes Beautiee?"

"Are you okay?"

"I'm worried about my father..." she sighed...

"Me too..."

"I can take the kids next door for a while if it'll help..." Theresa said...

"That will help... thanks..."

"How long are they gonna be here?" Charles asked...

"As long as it takes..." Bazil answered...

"What does that even mean?" Charles asked...

"Hell if I know..." Troy answered...

"We need to keep them out of school..." Bazil said...

"Why? Charles Jr. has nothing to do with this..." Charles said...

"He's in Amina's class – as soon as this gets out they'll pounce on the kids – especially since Ms. Shelby told Chandler my son saw the monsters in the backyard..." Bazil answered...

"Shit! Chandler – you can't take that out?" Charles asked...

"Are you really asking me that?" Chandler snapped...

"You're right – I'm sorry..."

"Let's go get this food – we'll figure this out after we eat..." Troy said...

"Welcome to McDonalds – may I take your order?" the cashier asked...

"We'll have eight happy meals, eight quarter pounder with cheese meals, and eight apple pies..."

"Okay! What drinks would you like?"

"Fruit punch for the happy meals, ginger ale for the other meals..." Bazil answered...

"You got it..." the cashier said as he went to prepare the order and they went to sit down...

"I'm gonna call Jeremy and see what's going on in Milford before we go to News 12..." Chandler said...

"Good idea – if somebody else says something, you won't sound crazy..." Charles laughed...

"I don't give a fuck how I sound..." Bazil said. Nobody else spoke. Troy rubbed the back of his head and then he put his hand under his chin...

"Mr. Osgood – your order's ready..." the cashier said...

"Thank you..." Bazil said as he got up and went to the counter...

"My wife read In The Arms Of A Gangster..." the cashier said as he bagged the food...

"What did she think?" Bazil asked...

"She loved it – and she loves both of you..."

'Thank you..." Bazil said as he picked up a bag of food...

"I'll get this one..." Charles said as he got up to get the other bag...

"We got the drinks..." Chandler said as he and Troy picked up the trays and they left the restaurant...

"McDonalds!" the kids squealed when they came back with all the food...

"Thank you, thank you, thank you..." we all said as they took the food out the bags...

"Y'all come sit at the table!" Keisha yelled...

"Okay!" they squealed as they all ran into the kitchen...

"I think we should keep the kids out of school..." Bazil said...

"I think that's a good idea..." I said...

"Fine with me – I can sleep later!" Starr laughed...

"We can always stop by the school and pick up their work..." Keisha said...

"Theresa – what do you think?" Charles asked...

"I don't really wanna keep Lil' Charles home from school – but if all the kids are here and they don't have to go, he won't wanna go anyway..." she answered...

"We're gonna go see Jeremy..." Chandler said...

"Do you have to go Chandler?" Starr asked...

"I have to go – but I'll be back..."

"Is my father going with you?"

"Yes Starr..." Bazil answered...

"I wish you didn't have to go..."

"Me too..." Bazil sighed...

"I'm going to go lay down for a bit – Starr – when you're ready to send the kids over, just knock..." Theresa said as she got up to leave...

"Okay..." Starr said...

"I'ma go too..." Charles said...

"We'll go wichall..." Keisha said...

"Thank you Keisha..." I said...

"Y'all come out and give your parents a hug – they leavin!" Chandler yelled...

"Bye Mommy! Bye Daddy! By Grandma! Bye Grandpa! By Uncle Troy! Bye Auntie Keisha! Bye Uncle Charles! Bye Auntie Theresa! Bye Uncle Bazil! Bye Auntie Beautiee!"

"Bye y'all..." Keisha laughed as we all hugged our babies...

"Starr?"

"Yes Beautiee?"

"Come here..." I said as I pulled her into a hug... "Your father is going to be okay..."

"I sure hope so..." she sighed and then we all left.

CHAPTER 9

"Hey Chandler – hey Mr. Osgood – hold on a sec..." Jeremy said as they walked in... "Oh hell no – what the fuck is going on?!"

"That's what we're here to talk to you about..." Bazil said...

"Oh shit – Chandler – take them in the back – I'll be there in a sec... Blake!"

"Yea Sarge?"

"I need you out here..."

"I'll be right out..." he answered as Jeremy headed to his office in the back...

"Mr. Osgood – can you shed some light on this? Are people crazy?" Jeremy asked as he sat in his chair...

"Which question would you like me to answer first?" Bazil sighed...

"Pick one..."

"People aren't crazy... but they will be..."

"Chandler – have you been getting calls about zombies fuckin' in the backyard?"

"Yea..."

"So... Mr. Osgood?"

"Yes?"

"Have you had any zombies fuckin' in your backyard?"

"I still have zombies fuckin' in my backyard..."

"Wait – still?"

"My parents have been fuckin' in my backyard for about a week..."

"How can you be so calm?"

"Don't let my demeanor fool you... my wife keeps me sane..." he answered as he took my hand...

"So... your parents have been fuckin' in your backyard... for about a week... and you're calm because your wife keeps you sane... ummm... Mr. Osgood?"

"Yes Sergeant?"

"Please... call me Jeremy..."

"Jeremy..."

"The only reason I don't think you're crazy right now... is because Chandler is here... unless..."

"Unless what?" Chandler asked...

"You're not here to have him committed... right?"

"Hell no!" Chandler snapped...

"In all my years of working in this department..."

"Jeremy – my parents came to ask for my help... and to warn me..."

"What? Why do they need your help? They're dead!"

"I swear to God if one more person tells me my parents are dead... I'm going to fuckin' explode..."

"I'm sorry... I know this is hard for you... but you gotta understand..."

"I'm not the one that needs to understand Jeremy..."

"Look – you need to listen to what my father has to say..." Chandler said...

"Alright, alright – Mr. Osgood – go ahead..."

"My parents told me we have to tell the Landscaping Corporation to stop producing their new fertilizer..."

"What's this got to do with fertilizer?" Jeremy asked...

"When you water your plants, there's an ingredient in the fertilizer that gets absorbed into the soil, wakes up the dead... and..."

"They can't stop fuckin'?" Jeremy asked...

"Yes..." Bazil answered...

"Who are you?" Jeremy asked as he turned to Troy and Keisha...

"I'm Troy – and this is my wife, Keisha..."

"I'm Sergeant Hurley – Jeremy – le'me ask you..."

"Yea then been in our backyard..." Keisha interrupted...

"Did you actually see them?"

"They didn't – but I did..." I interrupted...

"You actually saw the zombies – I mean his parents? In your backyard? Fuckin'?"

"We both did..."

"You both did? You and your husband?"

"Me and my son..."

"Oh my God – Mr. Osgood – I'm sorry – Chandler..."

"Jeremy – my parents warned me – they're coming..." Bazil interrupted...

"What – I mean – who's coming?"

"Zombies..."

"Oh shit!" Jeremy exclaimed... "Chandler – what are we gonna do?"

"We need to go to the press – we gotta let people know what's going on – we're already getting reports..." Chandler said...

"They won't listen to us!"

"They will – they'll have your word, mine, my father's, his wife, and theirs..." he said as he nodded towards Keisha and Troy...

"I'm Scott McGee, Anchor and Managing Editor, News 12 Westchester. We interrupt our regularly scheduled programming to bring you this report. We go live to Tara Rosenblum..."

"Thank you Scott. I'm here with a woman who wishes to remain anonymous... go ahead Maam..."

"They're fuckin' in my backyard!" she exclaimed...

"Excuse me – Maam?"

"The zombies – they're in my backyard – I called the police – they wouldn't come!"

"Maam – where are the zombies?"

"I'll show you..."

"Ladies and gentlemen – the following video should not be viewed by children..." Scott said as the video was played...

"Oh my God!" Starr exclaimed...

"Starr? What's wrong?" Theresa asked...

"Look!" she exclaimed and they continued watching...

"Is this in Connecticut?" Theresa asked...

"No – it's in Westchester!"

"Oh my God – I'm going to get Charles..." Theresa said as she ran to the door and snatched it open... "Charles – did you see it?"

"I saw it..."

"Maam – when was this video taken?" Tara asked...

"It was taken last night! I called the police – they said I'm crazy so my husband took this video!"

"Well Scott – there you have it – Erotic Zombies – back to you..."

"We'll continue to update you on this bizarre story as it develops. In the meantime – residents are being warned to lock your doors before dark and stay indoors after sunset. We now return to our regularly scheduled programming...

"I'm gonna calls News 12..." Chandler said as he picked up his phone...

"You've reached Gwen Edwards, News 12 Connecticut – how may I help you?"

"This is Sergeant Chandler Corbett of the Bridgeport Police..."

"Do you have a story for me Sergeant Corbett?"

"I need to see you right away – if you agree to see me – you'll get an exclusive..."

"Can you meet me at 28 Cross Street in Norwalk?"

"Give me 30 minutes..." Chandler said and then he hung up... "Let's go!" he said as we left the precinct...

"Nice to see you Sergeant Corbett – Mr. Osgood – how are you?" Gwen asked as she extended her hand to shake his...

"Nice meeting you – can we go inside?"

"All of you?"

"All of us..." Bazil answered...

"This must be big..." she said as she led them all inside...

"Bazil Osgood – I thought that was you!" Della Crews beamed when she saw him...

"Hello Della..."

"You two know each other?" Gwen asked...

"Bazil and I go way back... isn't that right Bazil?" Della answered...

"We've gotta go – they're here to give me an exclusive..." Gwen said...

"An exclusive! Okay then! Right this way!" Della beamed as she escorted us all to Gwen's office. Once we were inside, Bazil got up to close the door...

"What's going on?" Della asked...

"The sooner we give Gwen the exclusive, the sooner you'll find out..." Bazil answered before closing the door...

"Wow... ummm..." Gwen started to say...

"Are there any recording devices in here?" Bazil asked...

"I'd like to record this – unless you'd prefer to be off the record..."

"I don't mind being on the record – I just want to make sure the only one that has to hear what we say is us..." Bazil said...

"I'd like this to be on camera... if that's alright..."

"That's fine with me – is it fine with you guys?" Bazil asked...

"I didn't know we was gonna be on camera..." Keisha said...

"Is that a problem for you?" Gwen asked...

"I guess it's aiight..." she said...

"Okay – let's get started..." Gwen said as she set up the camera. Once it was set to record, she hurried back over to her seat...

"We're recording in five, four, three, two, one... Good evening – I'm Gwen Edwards, Reporter, News 12 Connecticut. Tonight I'm here with Bazil Osgood, President and CEO of Osgood Publishing to bring you an exclusive – Go ahead Mr. Osgood...

"Earlier this week, my son was woken out of his sleep by noise in my backyard...

"Was there a break in?"

"I looked out the window... and I saw... zombies..."

"Mr. Osgood – is this some type of publicity stunt?"

"Ms. Edwards – I wouldn't be sitting here with Sergeant Corbett of Bridgeport, Sergeant Hurley of Milford, my wife, or my neighbors if I were trying to get publicity – unless I was being arrested..."

"I'm sorry – you said you saw zombies..."

"Yes – I saw them out the window..."

"How did they get in your backyard?"

"They came up through the grass..."

"What where they doing there?"

"Once I went out into the backyard... I realized the zombies were my parents..."

"Your parents?"

"My parents were there to ask for my help... and to warn me..."

"What do your parents need your help with?"

"My parents need you to contact the Landscaping Corporation and tell them they need to stop producing their new fertilizer..."

"Why would your parents... wait a minute – are you saying this new fertilizer wakes up the dead?"

"Once you water your plants, there's an ingredient in the fertilizer and once that gets absorbed into the soil... it wakes up the dead... and..."

"What Mr. Osgood?"

"The zombies aren't able to control their sexual urges..." Bazil sighed...

"Oh my God..." Gwen said...

"We've started getting reports from residents in Milford claiming that they've seen zombies having sex in their backyard..." Sergeant Hurley said...

"I also took a couple of reports today in Bridgeport claiming the same thing..." Chandler said...

"We didn't actually see any zombies – but my husband could tell something went down in our backyard..." Keisha said...

"What's your name Maam?"

"I'm Keisha Cochran – this is my husband, Troy..."

"Mr. Cochran – what did you see when you went in your backyard?"

"It looked like something came up out the dirt..."

"Have you been in your backyard since?"

"No..."

"Mr. Osgood – you said your parents were there to ask for your help – and to warn you..."

"Yes..."

"What was the warning?"

"Zombies are coming..."

"I have a backyard – I like to entertain – do I need to be afraid?"

"They only come out at night – but after what I saw in Troy's backyard... you won't want to entertain..."

"This is Gwen Edwards, Reporter, News 12 Connecticut and you're watching an exclusive interview where we've just learned Erotic Zombies have been observed by residents here in Fairfield County..." she said before she turned off the camera... "Mr. and Mrs. Osgood, Sergeant Corbett, Sergeant Hurley, Mr. and Mrs. Cochran – I want to thank you for this exclusive..."

"You're welcome..." Chandler said...

"See yourselves out – I gotta run!" she yelled as she ran down the hall...

"That went better than I expected..." Bazil said...

"I can already see it..." Chandler sighed...

"So can I..." Jeremy said...

"Whachall see?" Keisha asked...

"The reports..." Chandler answered as we left...

"This is Della Crews, Anchor, News 12 Connecticut. We interrupt our regularly scheduled programming to bring you this exclusive. We now turn to Gwen Edwards..."

CHAPTER 10

"Sam!" Joselyn breathed as she hurried into his office...

"Joselyn – what's wrong?"

"I need you in the conference room..." she said and then she ran down the hall...

"What's going on?" Same asked as he hurried into the conference room and began watching News 12...

"Mommy!"

"Yes Chandler?"

"Grandpa's on tv with Grandma, Daddy, Uncle Troy, and Auntie Keisha!"

"He is? Where?"

"In my room Mommy – c'mon!" Chandler Jr. said as he pulled Starr by her hand and she hurried into their room...

74

'I need to get back Chandler..." Jeremy said...

"Alright – thanks Jeremy..."

"You too – and thank you Mr. and Mrs. Osgood...

"You're welcome..." Bazil said...

"Where we goin' now?" Keisha asked...

"I need to go to my office – I'm sure Sam's seen News 12 by now..." Bazil answered...

"We're going to the Holiday Inn..." Troy said...

"We are?" Keisha asked...

"We need to be close to Amina..."

"We could just take her home..."

"Let her stay..."

"Okay – where's my husband?" Keisha laughed...

"Bazil – did I see what I think I just saw?" Sam asked as we walked in...

"Sam – I need everyone in the conference room..." Bazil said as we went to our office, went inside, and closed the door...

"I need you..." he breathed as he leaned back against the door, pulled me into his arms, and held me...

"I'm right here..." I said as I kissed him... "I'm not going anywhere..."

"You're not afraid?"

"I was afraid... but once I found out they were your parents... I can't believe I'm actually going to say this..."

"Say it..."

"I actually felt relieved..."

"I wish I could feel relieved..."

"Bazil..." I said as I took his face in my hands... "You will..."

"How can you be so sure?"

"Because... you wouldn't be trying so hard to help your parents if you didn't think it was the right thing to do..."

"I love you..."

"I love you too..."

"Bazil – they're ready..." Sam said outside the door...

"We're on our way..." Bazil said. Bazil pulled me into a kiss, kissed me hard, opened the door, took my hand, and we went down the hall to the conference room...

"Good afternoon everyone..." Bazil greeted...

"Good afternoon..." everyone said in unison...

"By a show of hands – how many of you have seen News 12?" I looked around and a few hands went up... "For those of you who haven't seen News 12, I went there to give an exclusive interview to Gwen Edwards, along with Sergeant Corbett from Bridgeport, Sergeant Hurley from Milford, my wife, and my neighbors..."

"Oooohhh..." some of the employees murmured...

"I went to tell them my dead parents came back from the dead to ask for my help and to warn me…"

"Oh my God!" somebody yelled…"

"Excuse me?" Sheila asked…

"Yes Sheila?"

"Ummm… never mind – I don't even know what to say…"

"That's okay – I'll explain. My parents asked me to tell the Landscaping Corporation to stop producing their fertilizer…"

"Okay – now I know what to ask – why?" Sheila laughed along with everyone else…

"When you water your plants, there's an ingredient in the fertilizer that gets absorbed and it wakes up the dead…"

"Oh my God! You mean like zombies?" Shadajah asked…

"Yes…"

"I'm glad we don't live near a graveyard…" Shadajah said…

"They don't just show up in graveyards – they show up in parks… and backyards…"

"That's it – I'm tellin' Henley don't open that fertilizer – throw it out!" Sheila snapped…

"You may be able to get your money back from the Landscaping Corporation…"

"Uh uh! That's okay – the bag might get wet and I have a big backyard – oh nooo!" Sheila said…

"I have a question?" A'Licia said…

"Yes A'Licia?"

"Are we in danger?" Everyone got really quiet. Bazil waited a minute or so before answering...

"According to what my parents told me, they only come out at night... so to answer your question – I'd say no..."

"They? So it's not just your parents?"

"No – it's not – the police have already started taking reports..."

"I have a question?" Cheryl said...

"Yes Cheryl?"

"How do we know the zombies only come out at night?"

"I only know what my parents told me..."

"I can't believe I left Stamford Hospital for this..." A'Licia sighed...

"I understand how you feel A'Licia, and if you wish to resign at this time – I don't want to lose you – but I understand..."

"I'll come in as long as I don't see any zombies when I go out to lunch – you do have a lot of grass and plants on the property..."

"Oh yea! That's right!" a few of the employees agreed...

"Here's what we're doing – effective immediately – we will be open from 9 a.m. to 3 p.m. – or you can work 9 a.m. to 2 p.m. with no lunch – but we will be closed at 3 p.m. This will give you time to run errands, look after family, etc. How's that sound?"

"I like that..." somebody said...

"That's sounds good..." somebody else said...

"I have a question?" Cheryl said...

"Yes Cheryl?"

"Are we going to lose pay?"

"Nobody's going to lose pay..."

"Oh thank God!" she said...

"Are there any other questions?" Bazil asked as he looked around the room. No one said anything... "Okay – since there isn't any other questions – have a good afternoon – and since it's already 2:30 – you might as well leave for the day..."

"Okay!" one of the employees said as they jumped up from the table and ran out the conference room...

"My husband's gonna be so happy to see me this early!" another employee said as she got up and ran out...

"Sam?"

"Yes Bazil?"

"Come with me..." Bazil said as we walked out the conference room together with Joselyn, Shadajah, Sheila, and A'Licia following behind us. When we got to our office and went inside, they followed us inside too... "Ladies – if you don't mind – I need to speak to Sam privately...

"We don't know what to do..." Shadajah said...

"You can go home..." Bazil said...

"Do I come back tomorrow?"

"Yes Shadajah..."

79

"Is it okay if I tell my mother?"

"Absolutely..."

"Okay – bye!" she said and then she left...

"A'Licia and I were working on quarterly reports..." Sheila said...

"Those can wait..." Bazil said...

"Actually... they can't..."

"Sheila?"

"Yes Bazil?"

"Go home – you and A'Licia can finish the reports tomorrow..."

"Okay – goodnight – I'll see you tomorrow – A'Licia – you can go home too..."

"I am – bye!" she said as she hurried out and Sheila left behind her...

"I'll see you at home Sam..." Joselyn said...

"Babe – wait for me – we won't be long – right Bazil?"

"We won't be long..." Bazil acknowledged...

"Joselyn – come keep me company in the cafeteria..." I said...

"I'm not hungry..."

"Neither am I..." I said as I got up to leave and then we headed down the hall to the cafeteria...

"Are we okay?" Sam asked...

"That's what I need to find out..."

"I don't understand..."

"I want us to go check around the building and make sure everything's okay..."

"Okay..." Sam said as he got up...

"We also need to stop using that fertilizer..." Bazil said as he got up and they went outside and started walking around the building...

"Umm... Bazil?"

"Yea Sam?"

"You need to come see this..."

"Shit!"

CHAPTER 11

"Grandpa! Grandma! Auntie Keisha! Uncle Troy! Daddy! Mommy!"

"I'd say that covers it..." Bazil laughed...

"Daddy – I'm so glad you're okay..." Starr said as she pulled him into a hug...

"Starr... you're shaking..."

"I know..." she said as she started crying...

"Don't cry Starr – Daddy will make the monsters go away – right Daddy?" Jay asked as everyone got really quiet and Charles walked in...

"What'd I miss?" he asked...

"Daddy's gonna make the monsters go away so we don't have to be scared – right Daddy?" Jay asked again. I looked at Bazil and I knew he didn't want to answer Jay – but he knew he had to...

"Yes Jay – Daddy's gonna help make the monsters go away..."

"Yeeaaa!" they all squealed and then they ran down the hall...

"You just lied to my son..." Charles said...

"Charles – hold on a minute..." Chandler started to say but Charles interrupted him...

"Chandler – I'm sorry – but your father can't guarantee what he just said!"

"Charles!" Theresa snapped... "Would you rather he tell the kids the monsters won't go away?"

"He lied to my son – I don't care what you, Chandler, or anybody else has to say..."

"Wai' a min – you bein' a little too extra..." Keisha said...

"Keisha..." Troy said as he put his hand on her shoulder...

"Naaa Troy – he wasn't there..."

"I saw the interview – and so did the kids!" Charles exclaimed...

"Stop it!" Starr yelled...

"Starr – calm down – you'll upset the kids..." I said...

"I'm sorry Beautiee – but that's my father – he risked everything to do that interview – and so did Chandler – he doesn't care that people think he's crazy –he just wants to help – and you have no business calling my father a liar Charles..."

"Theresa – get Lil' Charles – we're leaving..." Charles said as he went towards the door..."

"That won't be necessary – I'll leave..." Bazil said...

"Nobody's going anywhere! We all stayin' here, the kids stayin' here – and we gonna get through this shit without arguing or calling anybody a liar – especially my father – understood?" Chandler snapped...

"We leavin' – y'all ain't got room for us anyway..." Keisha laughed...

"True dat..." Troy agreed...

"You can stay – we're going home – I need to keep an eye on the house..." Bazil said...

"Daddy – please... don't leave..." Starr pleaded...

"We can have dinner – then you can get the fuck out if ya want..." Chandler said...

"Chandler!' Starr snapped...

"I'm just playin'..." Chandler said as he pulled Starr into a hug and kissed her...

"We goin' to the Holiday Inn..." Keisha said...

"You know what – that's a good idea – we should all go to the Holiday Inn – y'all can get a room and then we can go to Park City Grill to eat..." Chandler said and then he yelled for the kids to get ready before anybody could object... "Y'all get in here!"

"Yes?" they all said as they line up...

"We goin' out to eat – get your clothes and shoes on..."

"Yeeaaa!" they all squealed and then they ran down the hall...

84

"We'll pass..." Charles said...

"Charles – we're going..." Theresa said...

"Theresa..." Charles started to say but Theresa walked up to Charles, took his face in her hands, kissed him, and said... "I said..." and then she kissed him again... "We're going..."

"Okay..." he sighed... "We'll go..."

"We'll meet you over there..." Bazil said as he got up and took my hand to help me up...

"We might as well leave with you..." Troy said as he got up and followed us along with Keisha and we left. When we got in the elevator, Keisha spoke...

"That was fucked up..."

"Keisha – it's fine..." Bazil said...

"No it's not – Starr's right – he didn't have to call you a liar..."

"Keisha – I'm doing everything I said I was going to do..."

"Exactly – so you're not a liar..."

"That's exactly my point..." Bazil said as we got off the elevator and went to get in our cars...

"Bazil... are you okay? Really?" I asked as he started the car...

"Charles has a bug up his ass – but it's his bug – his ass – not mine..." he answered as he picked up his phone and put it on speaker... "Hello Smalls – I can't talk now..."

"We have a problem..."

"Hi Smalls!" I beamed...

"Hi Beautiee – Bazil – we need to talk..."

"I'll call you later tonight..." Bazil said as he hung up and we headed downtown to the Holiday Inn...

"Mr. Osgood!" the reporters came running along with their cameras as soon as they saw us, giving Keisha and Troy an opportunity to run inside...

"When was the first time you saw your parents?"

"How long have your parents been zombies?"

"Have you always seen ghosts?"

"Are you psychic?"

"How many times have your parents visited?"

"Have you contacted the Landscaping Corporation?"

"Have you seen zombies during the day?"

"How do you know they can't control their sexual urges?"

"Mrs. Osgood – have you seen the zombies? We're you scared?" Bazil took me by the hand and started to pull me away from the cameras but when I started speaking he changed his mind...

"Yes, I've seen his parents in our backyard..." I answered as the cameras flashed...

"Were you scared?"

"I'm not afraid of his parents..." I answered...

"Were they having sex when you saw them?"

"Yes they were..." I answered as Chandler pulled up, opened the door, and the kids jumped out of the car...

"Uh uh! Get these cameras away from these kids!" Chandler yelled as we ran over to shield the kids. Troy and Keisha came running and pulled the kids inside the hotel...

"Y'all alright?" Keisha asked...

"I'm okay Mommy..." Amina answered...

"I'm fine..." Jay beamed...

"Y'all alright?" Chandler asked...

"Yes Daddy!" they answered in unison...

"Daddy!" Starr breathed as she ran over to Bazil and hugged him...

"I'm okay..."

"You okay Mommy?" Joseph asked...

"I'm fine – are you okay?" I asked as I went over to Joseph and Joy..."

"I'm okay Mommy..." Joy answered...

"We should'a never came out here..." Troy sighed...

"I'm sorry..." Bazil said...

"You don't have to apologize – you didn't know..." Troy said...

"What happened?" Charles asked a she came in with Theresa and Lil' Charles...

"Just some thirsty reporters tryin' to get a story – we good..." Chandler answered...

"How did they know we were here?" I asked...

"Keisha!" Troy exclaimed as she stormed over to the concierge area...

"May I help you?" the manager asked...

"Where's the lady that took our reservation?" Keisha snapped...

"Is there a problem?"

"Hell yea there's a fuckin' problem – she called the news and told them we were here – and now we got cameras and reporters outside tryin' to get a comment and they tried to get at our kids!" she snapped...

"Mrs. Cochran – I assure you – no one here would do something so irresponsible..."

"I ain't say you did it – I said she did it!" Keisha snapped...

"She's gone for the day – we'll look into this and she'll be dealt with – in the meantime, we'll credit you the charges for the room, and we'll take care of dinner for you and your family..." the manager said as he came out from behind the counter and went over to Park City Grill...

"Good evening – may I get you a table for one?" the hostess asked...

"No thank you – I'm here for them..." he said as he nodded towards us...

"You're here for the Osgoods?" she asked...

"I'm here for the Osgoods and their guests – when they're done with dinner, please charge their check to this card..." he said as he handed her a black card..."

"Yes sir..." she said as she came out from behind the podium and walked over to us...

"Good evening – welcome to Park City Grill – how many do we have in your party?" she asked...

"Sixteen..." Bazil answered...

"We can make that work – come with me..." she said as we followed her into the restaurant...

"Oh shoot – that's Mr. Osgood!" someone said...

"Hi Beautiee!" Somebody else said...

"Hello..." I said as I smiled and waived...

"I like when you get ganster..." Troy said as he pulled Keisha into a kiss and then they sat down...

"Had to check 'em..." Keisha said...

"Thank you..." Bazil said as we sat down...

"I wanna sit by Daddy!" Jay said...

"I'll move over so you can sit by Daddy..." I said as I got up to move...

"No Beautiee – Jay, Joseph, Joy – you sit right across from us over there..."

"Amina – you sit across from us next to them..." Keisha said...

"Okay!" Amina beamed as she sat down across from Keisha...

"I wanna sit here!" Chandler Jr. said as he ran to the table...

"No – I wanna sit there!" Chelsea said...

"Y'all don't have to fight – there's enough seats..." Chandler laughed as Chandler Jr., Chelsea, and Kalliyah sat down across from them...

"I wanna sit by Daddy – Daddy you sit there and I'll sit over here – Mommy you sit there..." Lil' Charles said...

"Okay..." Charles laughed as they sat where they were told...

"Is everybody comfortable?" the hostess said as she came over...

"Yeesss!" the kids all answered in unison...

"Your server will be over to bring you menus – can I do anything else for you?"

"No – we're okay..." Theresa said...

"Welcome to Park City Grill – here's your menus – can I start you off with something to drink?"

"Fruit punch for them – ginger ales for us..." I laughed...

"Ginger ales?" Keisha asked...

"Well... we haven't had anything to eat yet..." I answered...

"We'll have Pepsi..." Theresa said...

"Me too..." Starr said...

"Okay – I'll bring the fruit punch first..." the server said and then he went to get the fruit punch...

"The only thing they have on here for the kids is ravioli..." Starr said...

"You mean..." Theresa started to say...

"Shhh!" Starr said...

"Why are you sshhing me?" Theresa laughed...

"Because if you say it they won't eat it..." Starr laughed...

"I'll eat it!" Chelsea said...

"You'll eat what?" Chandler laughed...

"Coconut shrimp..."

"When you had coconut shrimp?"

"I tasted it when Mommy made it – and it was good..."

"I want some coconut shrimp!" Jay said...

"Me too!" Amina said...

"You ain't never had no coconut shrimp!" Keisha laughed...

"Chelsea said it was good..." Amina said...

"I can't..." Troy laughed...

"I'm getting the salmon..." Theresa said...

"Yuck!" Starr laughed...

"I guess you don't like Salmon..." Charles laughed...

"I sure don't!" Starr laughed...

"I'ma have the twin pork chops..." Keisha said...

"I'm getting spaghetti Bolognese..." Starr said...

"I'ma go with the Delmonico steak..." Chandler said...

"I'm getting the NY strip steak..." Troy said...

"I'm getting the filet mignon..." Bazil said...

"I'm going with the chicken saltimbocca..." Charles said...

"Beautiee – what are you getting?" Bazil asked...

"I'm gonna get the linguini & shrimp..." I answered...

"Here's your fruit punch..." the server said as he put two pitchers of fruit punch on the table... "Here's your ginger ale..." he said as he put two pitchers of ginger ale on our end of the table... "And here's your Pepsi..." he said as he put two pitchers of Pepsi at the other end of the table... "Are you ready to order?"

"Two order of coconut shrimp and 8 orders of mushroom ravioli..." Bazil said...

"Ewww! I don't want any mushrooms!" Jay said...

"Try it – if you don't like the mushrooms – just eat the ravioli..." I said...

"We can make it without the mushrooms if you prefer..." the server said...

"Thank you – please do that..." I said...

"I'll go put the order in for your appetizers..."

"Those are for the kids – not us!" I laughed...

"Okay – I'll go place the order so they can get started – I'll be back..." the server said as Keisha got up and started pouring fruit punch. Theresa got up and poured fruit punch for the kids at the other end of the table just as the server came back...

"Okay – what's everybody having?"

"Salmon, pork chops, spaghetti Bolognese, Delmonico steak, NY strip steak, filet mignon, chicken saltimborca, and linguini with shrimp..." Theresa answered...

"Got it!" the server said as he went to place the order..."

"Damn that was good!" Troy exclaimed!"

"Sure was!" Keisha agreed...

"I'm stuffed..." Bazil said...

"I'm good now..." I said...

"My salmon was delicious!" Theresa said...

"So was my chicken..." Charles said...

"I'm glad they had spaghetti Bolognese..." Starr said...

"I'm tired Mommy..." Amina yawned...

"Uh huh – y'all done ate yourselves sleepy..." Troy laughed...

"We need to get going – it's getting dark..." Bazil said as he got up..."

"C'mon y'all..." Chandler said as he got up along with the kids and everyone else. After we all got in the lobby of the hotel, we hugged, kissed, Troy and Keisha went to the elevator, and Bazil went to look out the door...

"We good?" Chandler asked...

"Yea – they're gone..."

"Okay – let's go!" Chandler said as the kids followed Chandler outside to the car. Bazil and I went outside and waited for Chandler to pull off before we started walking towards our car...

"Good night y'all..." Theresa said...

"Good night – we'll see you soon..." Bazil said as he opened the door for me to get in. Once we were in the car, we started driving down Main

Street towards McLevy Green and when we got to McLevy Green that's when I saw them...

"Bazil – stop the car!"

"Oh shit!" Bazil exclaimed as we saw two female zombies holding onto the back of the bench as two males were pounding them from behind.

"I'm calling Chandler..." Bazil said as he picked up his phone and dialed...

"Hi Dad – y'all home already?"

"Chandler – they're at McLevy Green..."

"What?"

"We just saw them..."

"How many?"

"Two males, two females..."

"Thanks Dad..." Chandler said as he hung up...

"Chandler – where are you going?" Starr exclaimed...

"I gotta go – I'll explain when I get back..." he said as he ran out the door...

"Sarge – I thought you were off tonight..." Officer Blake said...

"They're in the park!" Chandler exclaimed...

"What? Which one?"

"McLevy Green!" Chandler snapped as he ran out the door and the other officers followed behind him...

"I'll find out what's going on myself..." Starr said as she turned on the scanner...

"Attention all units – zombies have been spotted in McLevy Green..."

"Copy that – Sergeant Corbett from Bridgeport responding..."

"Chandler..." Starr whispered...

"This is Della Crews, News 12 Connecticut. Earlier this evening, the Osgoods were spotted going into the Holiday Inn, where we were able to get a few comments from Mrs. Osgood..."

"Mrs. Osgood – have you seen the zombies? We're you scared?"

"Yes, I've seen his parents in our backyard..."

"Were you scared?"

"I'm not afraid of his parents..."

"Were they having sex when you saw them?"

"Yes they were..."

"Uh uh! Get these cameras away from these kids!"

"What's that? Hang on...we've just been notified that Erotic Zombies have been spotted at

McLevy Green, downtown Bridgeport. Gwen Edwards is live on the scene – Gwen – what can you tell us?"

"Della – it's crazy – as you can see behind me – officers are attempting to block the area by taping it off as some of the officers are fighting off the zombies..."

"Did you say fighting? The officers are actually fighting?"

"The officers are attempting to block the zombies from leaving and the zombies are attempting to push back – oh shit..."

"Gwen? Gwen are you there? We've lost contact – we'll be back momentarily – we'll keep you posted..."

"Sarge..."

"What the hell? Thompson?"

"Yea..."

"What the hell – never mind – I'm not talkin' to you – you're dead!"

"I'm sorry..."

"Get the fuck outta here!" Chandler snapped...

"You think I wanna be here?"

"Why the hell are you here?"

"Bazil already told you..."

"Wait a minute..."

"Sarge – hurry – before it's too late!" Jermoll said and then he went back in the dirt along with the other zombies...

"Bazil – you're in trouble..." Smalls said...

"I know..."

"Bazil – listen..."

"Okay..."

"I got a call from the Landscaping Corporation..."

"Oh shit..."

"They wanted me to represent them but I told them I represent you..."

"So they're coming for me?"

"They're coming for you..."

"I kinda figured they would..."

"Bazil – they're going to bankrupt you..."

"I'm willing to take that risk..."

"Bazil – why?"

"Because my parents need me..."

"Bazil... your parents..."

"Don't fuckin' say it..."

"I'm sorry..."

"I'll see you in court if I have to..."

"I'm praying it doesn't come to that..."

"Me too..."

"I'll keep you posted..." Smalls said before he hung up...

"Is it bad?" I asked, already knowing the answer...

"It's bad..." Bazil sighed as he pulled me into a hug and we held each other...

"I made you a promise earlier..." I whispered...

"Yes... you did..."

'I'd like to keep that promise..."

"I'd like that too..."

"Come with me..." I said as I took him by the hand and led him into the living room... "Sit..." I commanded. Bazil sat down on the couch and smiled at me mischievously. I stood there looking at him for a few moments before I moved closer to him and stood in front of him. Bazil reach up and grabbed me by my hips and then I spoke... "Don't..." Bazil put his hands down and smiled as I grabbed the pillows on the end of the couch, dropped them on the floor, kneeled on them, and spread his legs...

"Yeesss..." he breathed as I unbuckled his belt and unzipped his pants. Instead of taking his dick out with my hands and stroking it, I put my head between his legs and tortured him by moving his dick around with my tongue before taking it in my mouth...

"Bazil! ¿Qué estás haciendo? Bazil! What are you doing?" his mother whispered...

"Shhh..." his father whispered as she came closer and they peeked through the window...

"Dios mío, ¿deberíamos dejar que terminen? Oh my God – should we let them finish?"

"Ojalá pudiéramos ... pero nos estamos quedando sin tiempo ... I wish we could.... but we're running out of time..."

"Me recuerda a nosotras ... Reminds me of us..." his mother laughed...

"Lo sé, sería muy tranquilo ... comenzarías a chuparme la polla ... ¡y BAM! ¡Aquí había venido tocando a la puerta! I know – it would be so quiet... you'd start suckin' my dick... and BAM! – here he'd come knocking on the door!" his father laughed...

"Hmmm, eso me da una idea ... Hmmm – that gives me an idea..." she said as she knelt down and took his dick out his pants...

"Mi Lydia ... tus manos ... se sienten tan bien ... Mi Lydia... your hands... they feel so good..."

"¿Cómo se siente esto? How does this feel?" she asked as she took his dick in her mouth...

"Mi Lydia... Oooohhh...." he moaned as he grabbed her head with his hands and fucked her mouth. He was moaning so loud he probably woke up the entire neighborhood – but he didn't care – this was the first time he'd felt his wife's mouth since they died – and in that moment he wasn't in his son's backyard – he was in heaven... "Mi Lydia - ¡Soy CUUMMIINNGG! Mi Lydia – I'M CUUMMIINNGG!" he boomed as his body convulsed...

"Me sabes tan bien ... You taste so good to me..." she breathed as she continued sucking for a few moments and then he started crying... "Me sabes tan bien ... Bazil... my love... no..." she whispered as she stood up, wrapped her arms around him, and held him... "Te amo ... por favor no llores ... I love you... please don't cry..."

"Mi Lyida ... me haces sentir tan bien ... Quiero quedarme aquí para poder sentirte por siempre ... Mi Lydia... you make me feel so good... I want to stay here so I can feel you forever..."

"Bazil ... mi amor ... me sentirás por siempre ... Bazil... my love... you will feel me forever..." she breathed as she pulled him into a kiss...

"Mi Lydia ... te amo ... Mi Lydia... I love you..."

"Bazil ... yo también te amo ... Bazil... I love you too..."

"Tenemos que decirles ahora ... We have to tell them now..."

"Si... Yes..." she said as they moved over to the French doors and started knocking...

"Beautiee..." he moaned as he grabbed my head and pushed his dick in further...

"Mmm... hhmmm..." I moaned on his dick as he fucked my mouth..."

"Tick... tick... tick..."

"Bazil..."

"Yes... Beautiee..." he moaned...

"What's that noise?"

"Tick... tick... tick..."

"Let me go check..." Bazil said as he jumped up and went to the kitchen. When he didn't come back right away, I knew it wasn't good...

"Mom... Dad..." Bazil said as he opened the French doors..."

"Bazil... I'm sorry..." his father said as Bazil stepped out into the backyard. I walked into the kitchen and stood by the door so I could continue to hear their conversation...

"What's wrong?" Bazil asked...

"We ran out of time..." his mother said as she started crying...

"Mi Lydia ... por favor no llores ..."

"Mi Lydia... please don't cry..." his father said as he wiped her tears...

"I did what you said..." Bazil said a she started crying...

"Yes... you did... but it's too late..." his father said...

"Tell me what to do... let me try and fix it..." Bazil cried... "Please..." At this point, I started crying too...

"Clayton always wanted me..." his mother said...

"I don't understand..." Bazil said...

"He tried to force me to be with him... but your father took care of that..."

"You killed him?" Bazil asked...

"Yes..." his father answered...

"Once he was dead... we were free to live our lives... we were happy... we had you... and we could be together in eternity... as long as he was dead... but now..." his mother said and then she started crying again...

"Mom..."

"Mi Lydia..." his father whispered as he took her face in his hands and kissed her...

"He's awake..." Bazil sighed...

"It's not just that..." she said as she continued crying...

"Clayton is angry..." his father said...

"He's coming for you... isn't he?" Bazil asked...

"He's coming for both of us..." his mother cried...

"What can I do?" Bazil asked...

"Clayton is the Alpha..." his father answered...

"What does that even mean?"

"It means he's controlling all the other zombies – including your parents..." I answered as I stepped outside into the backyard...

"Beautiee..." Bazil whispered...

"Beautiee – I'm so sorry..." his mother cried...

"Beautiee – don't!" Bazil yelled as he tried to stop me from hugging his mother...

"You're not afraid of me?" she asked...

"No..." I answered as we hugged each other...

"Dad..." Bazil cried as he ran to hug his father...

"Hello Bazil..." his father said as Bazil cried in his father's arms... "Stop crying and go hug your mother..." he laughed. Bazil came over to hug his mother and I went to hug his father...

"I've wanted to do this ever since I saw you... but I was afraid..." Bazil cried...

"We'd never hurt you..." his mother said...

"We'll do whatever it takes..." I said...

"I know you will – I've seen what you're capable of..." Bazil's father laughed...

"I wish we got to know you before we died..." his mother said...

"So do I..." I said...

"As happy as I am to be having this reunion, we need to talk..." his father said...

"What's wrong?" Bazil asked...

"Clayton is close..."

"Oh damn..."

"The other zombies are a distraction..." his mother said...

"He wants to eliminate me... so he can have your mother in eternity..." his father said...

"How can he eliminate you?" Bazil asked...

"By crushing my skull..."

"I won't let that happen..." Bazil gritted...

"He's too strong... you can't fight him..." his mother said...

"Yes... we can..." I said...

"Beautiee – you don't understand..."

"Lydia – we got this..." I said...

"See Lydia – I knew I was right about her..." Bazil's father said...

"Beautiee – I love you – but I'm scared for you..." his mother said...

"We'll be alright..." I said...

"My grandchildren need you..." she said...

"And I'll be there for them..."

"Damn I love you..." Bazil said as he pulled me into a kiss and kissed me hard...

"I miss you so much Mommy..." Denise said as she placed the flowers on her mother's grave. Denise kneeled down on the ground, sat down, leaned against the tombstone, pulled out Beautiee's book, and started reading...

"I'm Scott McGee, Anchor and managing Editor, News 12 Westchester. We've just received word that Erotic Zombies have been spotted in Oakland Cemetery. We now go to Tara Rosenblum at Oakland Cemetery – Tara – what can you tell us?"

"Scott – I can't go anywhere near the entrance – can you see what's going on behind me?"

"Tara... is that what I think it is?"

"Yes Scott – the zombies are wreaking havoc, running around... and having sex..."

"Oh shit! I gotta go!" Titus yelled as he jumped up...

"Daddy! Where are you going?"

"I'm going to get your mother!" he yelled as he snatched the door open and ran out the house...

"What the... damn. I didn't mean to fall asleep – oh shit – what the..."

"Ssshhh..." her mother whispered as she pulled Denise down and covered her mouth...

"Get your hands off... Mommy?"

"Yes – be quiet!" she whispered as she pulled Denise back down on the dirt and covered her mouth...

"Wait a minute – I'm getting something..." Tara said as she hurried over to the entrance... "Sir – you can't go in there..."

"My wife's in there!" Titus snapped...

"I'm sorry - when did your wife die?"

"She didn't die – she went to go visit her mother – I need to find her!"

"Scott – we're going in..." Tara said as she took off her shoes, threw them, and ran behind Titus...

"Denise! Where are you?"

"Titus! I'm here!" she yelled...

"I'm coming!" Titus yelled as he ran with Tara and the cameras following behind him...

"Denise!" he breathed as he pulled her up off the ground into his arms...

"Titus!" she cried... "Oh thank God!"

"What are you still doing here?"

"I fell asleep..."

"I'm Tara Rosenbloom..."

"I know who you are..." Denise beamed...

"Are you okay Maam?"

"I"m okay – my mother..." she started to say before she burst into tears...

"Your mother? Where's your mother?" Tara asked...

"She was here..."

"Your mother was here?" Titus asked...

"She pulled me down and protected me..."

"Oh wow... that's beautiful..." Tara said as she wiped her tears...

"Let's go – these zombies are crazy!" Titus said...

"Scott – did you get that?" Tara asked...

"We got it Tara..." Scott said as they hurried out the cemetery...

CHAPTER 13

"I can't wait to get upstairs and hug my wife and kids..." Chandler said out loud as he parked his car. When he got out and started walking to the entrance to his building, that's when he heard Jermoll calling...

"Sarge..."

"Naa – I know I must be tired..."

"Sarge!"

"Oh hell no!" Chandler snapped...

"Sarge – you gotta help me!"

"Yo – get the fuck outta here!" Chandler yelled as he walked towards the grass and bushes behind the parking lot with his gun drawn...

"That won't work..." Jermoll said...

"What the fuck are you talking about?" Chandler snapped. Chandler was unaware that the doorman followed him and was watching and listening...

"Sarge... I don't wanna be here..."

"So leave!" Chandler snapped...

"I can't leave... unless you crush my skull..."

"Why me? Why didn't you ask one a them?"

"They kept shooting... they wouldn't listen..."

"I'm not listening either..."

"Sarge! Just pick up that rock... make it quick... and I'll be gone..."

"I can't do it Jermoll..."

"Sarge... please..."

"I'ma turn around... I'ma go upstairs... I'ma kiss my wife... I'ma kiss my kids... and I'ma act like I didn't see you..." Chandler said as he turned to walk away... "Noooo!" Chandler yelled as he tried to stop the doorman but couldn't... Bam! Bam! Bam!

"Blake..." Chandler called on his radio...

"Yea Sarge?"

"We need a unit... and a body bag..."

"Where?"

"My parking lot..." Chandler sighed...

"Mr. Chandler..."

"Go inside... and stay there..."

"Yes Sir Mr. Chandler..." the doorman said as he walked back to the entrance of the complex and Chandler took out his cell phone...

"Starr..."

"I know..."

"You know?"

"I've been listening to the scanner..."

"I'll be upstairs as soon as we're done..."

"I can't wait for us to go to bed..."

"Oh yea?"

"Yea..."

"Okay! I hear you – le'me go – I'll see you in a bit..."

"I love you..."

"I love you too..." Chandler said as he hung up...

"You good Sarge?' Blake asked as he hurried over to where Chandler was standing...

"I'm good..."

"Oh shit! What happened?"

"Looks to me like somebody took out a zombie..." Chandler laughed...

"You sure it's a zombie?"

"It's a zombie – look at the decomposer of the body..."

"You're right – I wonder what it was doing here?"

"Who knows?" Chandler answered as the ambulette pulled up...

"Hey Sarge – how many we got?"

"We got one..."

"Oh shit – I guess we don't have to worry about this one..." the tech laughed as he bagged Jermoll's body...

"We sure don't" Blake laughed...

"Okay – we got it – we'll get this over to the crematorium..." the tech said as he put

Jermoll's body in the ambulette, closed the door, jumped in the driver's seat, and drove off...

"Okay Sarge – if you need me..."

"I know, I know..."

"Good night..."

"Good night..." Chandler said as he went upstairs. When he got inside, Starr took him by the hand and led him into the bedroom...

"Where's the kids?" he asked as he took off his holster, put it on the dresser, and began to take off his clothes...

"They're sleeping..." she whispered as she dropped her robe and climbed into bed...

"This is Della Crews, News 12 Connecticut. Earlier this evening, we were bringing you live coverage with Gwen Edwards in downtown Bridgeport. Zombies were spotted on McLevy Green and as officers were attempting to block the area, Gwen lost her connection due to technical issues. At the same time, we contacted the Landscaping Corporation, and Liam, President, issued the following statement:

"We are sorry to learn that our fertilizer is responsible for these recent incidents. As of today, we have stopped producing the fertilizer. All fertilizer has been removed from stores in Westchester County as well as Fairfield Counties. Anyone that still has fertilizer is encouraged to either reach out to the Landscaping Corporation directly to have it picked up and disposed of or to return it to the store where it was purchased for a full refund. Please - DO NOT throw the fertilizer in garbage cans..."

"I'm Della Crews, News 12 Connecticut. We'll continue to bring you updates..."

"Good morning Mrs. Osgood..." Bazil breathed as he kissed me awake..."

"Mmmm... good morning..." I breathed...

"What would you like for breakfast?" he asked as he began kissing me on my neck...

"I'd like dessert..." I breathed as I arched my back...

"Cumming right up..." he breathed and then he put his tongue in my mouth, climbed on top of me, and spread my legs... "Shit!"

"Is... that... your... phone?" I breathed between kisses...

"Mmmm hmmmm...."

"Answer it..."

"No..."

"It... could... be... important..."

"This is important..." he breathed as he eased himself inside me...

"Bazil... Huh..."

"Yes... Beautiee..." Bazil thrust his tongue in my mouth and started thrusting harder...

"Mmmm... Mmmm... Mmmm..."

"Mmmph... Mmmph... Mmmph..."

"Mmmm... Mmmm... Mmmm..."

"Mmmph... Mmmph... Mmmph..." I grabbed Bazil's ass, spread my legs, and pushed him in deeper...

"Bazil... Fuck... I'm cumming..."

"Cum for me..." he growled...

"Haah... Haah... Haah... Haaaaahhhh!"

"Uuugh! Uuugh! Uuugh! Uuuuggghhhh!"

"I needed that..." I breathed...

"I know..." he breathed as he kissed my neck...

"It's been so long since we've been able to fuck without being interrupted..."

"I know..." he breathed as he continued kissing my neck...

"I need to do this more often..."

"Mmmm... sounds good..." he breathed as he kissed me... "Shit!"

"Answer it..."

"No..."

"Bazil..."

"No..."

"It could be the kids..."

"Okay..." Bazil said as he picked up the phone...

"Good morning..."

"Bazil – I've been trying to call you..."

"Do we have a court date?"

"Have you seen News 12?"

"Not since last night..."

"Turn on News 12..."

"Okay..." he said as he got up to turn on the television...

113

"This is Della Crews, News 12 Connecticut. Earlier this evening, we were bringing you live coverage with Gwen Edwards in downtown Bridgeport. Zombies were spotted on McLevy Green and as officers were attempting to block the area, Gwen lost her connection due to technical issues. At the same time, we contacted the Landscaping Corporation, and Liam, President, issued the following statement:

"We are sorry to learn that our fertilizer is responsible for these recent incidents. As of today, we have stopped producing the fertilizer. All fertilizer has been removed from stores in Westchester County as well as Fairfield Counties. Anyone that still has fertilizer is encouraged to either reach out to the Landscaping Corporation Corporation directly to have it picked up and disposed of or to return it to the store where it was purchased for a full refund. Please - DO NOT throw the fertilizer in garbage cans..."

"I'm Della Crews, News 12 Connecticut. We'll continue to bring you updates..."

"Is this for real?" Bazil asked...
"It's real..."
"Thank you..."
"You're welcome..."
"I don't believe it..." I said...
"Neither do I..."

"I can't wait to tell your parents..."

"We did it!" Bazil said as he pulled me up into his arms and kissed me...

"You did it..."

"Let's go have breakfast – then we'll go see the kids...

"Okay..."

"Chandler... Huh... Huh..."

"Ummph... Ummph... Ummph..."

"Chan – no... don't wake them up..." Jay whispered...

"I be right back – I go pee pee..."

"Chandler... I'm cumming... Haa... Haa... Haa... Haa... Haaaaa!"

"Starr... Fuck... Uuugh! Uuugh! Uuuggghhh!"

"Waaaahhhh!" Lil Chandler cried as he ran back in the room...

"What's wrong Chan?" Jay asked as Joseph, Joy, and Amina sat up, rubbing their eyes...

"Don't cry Chan..." Chelsea said as she got up out the bed to hug him...

"Daddy hurt Mommy!"

"Daddy hurt Mommy?" Kalliyah asked as she jumped up out the bed...

"Daddy loves Mommy Chan..." Chelsea said, trying to reassure him...

"No!" Chandler Jr. snapped as he pushed his sisters away from him and got on the floor... "Daddy hurt Mommy like this..." he cried and then he mimicked Chandler on top of Starr... "Uuugh! Uuugh! Uuugh!"

"He didn't hurt Starr – he was playin'" Jay said...

"Daddy was playin'?" Chandler Jr. asked as he got up and wiped his eyes...

"Uh huh – I see Mommy and Daddy playin' all the time..." Jay giggled...

"You do?" Chandler Jr. asked...

"Mommy and Daddy play... and then Mommy gets a baby in her tummy..."

"Ooohhh..." Chandler Jr. exclaimed as his eyes got really big...

"My Mommy don't play with my Daddy..." Amina said...

"Yes she does Amina – that's how you got in her tummy..." Jay said...

"Uh uh – my Mommy don't play with my Daddy 'cause my Mommy always tell my Daddy she don't want no more damn kids!" Amina laughed.

CHAPTER 14

"Good morning Mr. Osgood, good morning Mrs. Osgood – would you like to order from the menu or will you be eating from the buffet?" the server asked...

"We'll be eating from the buffet..." Bazil answered...

"Would you like coffee?"

"Yes please..." I answered...

"I'll bring you a fresh pot of coffee..." she said and then she went to get our coffee...

"This morning was necessary..." Bazil said as he pulled me into a kiss...

"It was..."

"I'd forgotten what it was like to be just the two of us..."

"We didn't have to be quiet..." I laughed...

"You've never been quiet..." Bazil laughed...

"I can't help it..."

"Here's your coffee – enjoy your breakfast..." the server said as she placed a pot of coffee and two mugs on the table...

"C'mon – let's go get a plate before the corned beef hash is gone..." I said as I jumped up from the table and hurried over to the buffet. Bazil came up behind me with a plate in his hand and whispered in my ear...

"I see you're hungry..."

"Bazil! Stop it!" I laughed...

"What if I don't?"

"I'll take you in one of these rooms..."

"Promise?"

"Excuse me – some of us are hungry!" a guest of the hotel snapped as he came and stood near us. Bazil and I looked at each other and bust out laughing...

"Is everything okay over here?" the server asked as she came over...

"It would be – if they'd move!" the guest snapped...

I'm sure the Osgoods wouldn't mind if you went around them..."

"C'mon honey – let's hurry up and get our plates..." I said as I put as much food on my plate as it would hold. Bazil did the same and we went back to the table...

"Mmmm... this is good..." Bazil said as he deliberately took his time putting his food in his mouth and licked his fork as he pulled it out his mouth...

118

"You're right... it is good..."

"Are you talking about the food... or me?" he asked, smiling mischievously...

"Both..." I answered as I put the fork in my mouth, pulling it out and licking it...

"I'd like you to finish what you started last night..."

"I'd like that too..."

"And I'd like to return the favor..."

"I'd love that..." I sighed...

"Can I get you anything else?" the server asked as she came over to the table...

"No thank you..." Bazil answered...

"Here's your check — you can pay it when you're ready..." she said as she placed the check down on the table...

"Let's go..." Bazil said as he got up and extended his hand to help me up...

"Good morning Dad, good morning Beautiee..." Chandler said as he opened the door...

"Good morning Daddy, good morning Beautiee..." Starr said...

"Good morning..." we both said in unison...

"Mommy! Daddy! Grandma! Grandpa! Uncle Bazil! Auntie Beautiee!" they squealed when they saw us...

"Where's my Daddy?" Amina asked...

"We right here..." Keisha said as they came inside...

"Good morning Troy, Keisha..." Chandler said...

"Good morning y'all..." Troy said...

"Daddy!" Amina squealed as she ran to Troy...

"How's my baby girl?" Troy asked as he picked her up and kissed her...

"I'm fine – I want Mommy..." she said as she held out her arms for Keisha...

"Aww... you miss Mommy?" Keisha asked as she took Amina from Troy...

"Mommy I wanna go home..."

"You can come home if you want..." Keisha said...

"Okay Mommy..."

"Daddy – can we go home?" Joseph asked...

"Not yet..." Bazil answered...

"How come?"

"Because Daddy and Mommy have to work..." Jay answered...

"But I wanna go home too..." Joy said...

"You'll come home soon..." I said... "Come give me a hug – we have to go to work...

"You coming back?" Joseph asked...

"Yes Joseph..."

"You promise?" he asked with tears in his eyes..."

"Come here..." Bazil said as he got down on his knees and extended his arms. Jay, Joseph, and Joy ran into their father's arms and he embraced them... "We're going to work... and then we're coming back... I promise..."

120

"Okay Daddy..." Joseph sighed...

"Who's my big boy?"

"Jay..."

"And?"

"Me?"

"Yes – you – and I need you to help Jay take care of your sister while we're at work – okay?"

"Okay Daddy..."

"Grandchildren front and center!" Bazil boomed. Chelsea, Kalliyah, and Chandler Jr. hurried to line up and salute... "On your mark, get set... hugs!" The children ran to hug Bazil and we all laughed as they knocked him down...

"Sorry Grandpa – you okay?" Chelsea asked...

"Sorry Grandpa..." Chandler Jr. said...

"C'mon Grandpa – take my hand..." Kalliyah said as she tried to pull Bazil up...

"C'mon – I'll help you..." I said as I tried to help Bazil up and he pulled me to the floor...

"Grandpa's playing with Grandma like Daddy was playing with Mommy – are you gonna get a baby in your tummy Grandma?"

"Daddy was playing with Mommy?" I asked as Chandler and Starr blushed...

"Uh huh..." Chandler Jr. Beamed...

"I see..." Bazil laughed as he got up and then he helped me up...

"C'mon y'all – we gon' get breakfast..." Chandler said...

"We might as well get going – we'll be back later – bye y'all!" Keisha said...

"Bye y'all" Troy said...

"Have a good day – we love you..." Bazil said...

"Love you too!" they all said in unison...

"Starr – come walk us out..." I said as I waited for her to come over to the door...

"I'm so embarrassed..." she whispered...

"I know exactly how you feel – remember?" I laughed...

"You're never gonna let me forget that – are you?"

"Probably not..." I laughed as we left...

"Hello?" Denise answered as she picked up her phone...

"Girl – turn on News 12!" her sister Rose said...

"Oh Shit – Titus – look!" Denise squealed as she jumped up and down...

"Oh shit! Y'all on News 12!" her son Anthony said as he answered his phone...

"Hello? I know, I know – I'm watching it now!" he told his cousin Tiannah..."

"Hello?" Malexus answered as she ran into the living room with her phone in her hand...

"Where's your mother?" her Aunt Monique asked...

"We watchin' it!"

"Call us back!" Tiannah said before Malexus hung up...

"I'm Scott McGee, Anchor and Managing Editor, News 12 Westchester. We've just received work that Erotic Zombies have been spotted in Oakland Cemetery. We now go to Tara Rosenblum at Oakland Cemetery – Tara – what can you tell us?"

"Scott – I can't go anywhere near the entrance – can you see what's going on behind me?"

"Tara... is that what I think it is?"

"Yes Scott – the zombies are wreaking havoc, running around... and having sex – wait a minute – I'm getting something...Sir – you can't go in there..."

"My wife's in there!"

"I'm sorry - when did your wife die?"

"She didn't die – she went to go visit her mother – I need to find her!"

"Scott – we're going in..."

"Denise! Where are you?"

"Titus! I'm here!"

"I'm coming! Denise!"

"Titus! Oh thank God!"

"What are you still doing here?"

"I fell asleep..."

"I'm Tara Rosenbloom..."

"I know who you are..."

"Are you okay Maam?"

"I"m okay – my mother..."

"Your mother? Where's your mother?"

"She was here..."

"Your mother was here?"

"She pulled me down and protected me..."

"Oh wow... that's beautiful..."

"Let's go – these zombies are crazy!"

"Scott – did you get that?"

"We got it Tara... I'm Scot McGee, Anchor and Managing Editor, News 12 Westchester. We'll continue to bring you updates..."

"Look at Dad bein' all cool n shit!" Anthony said...

"I know they gonna be hatin' when they see us! Mom – you weren't scared?" Malexus asked...

"Hell yea I was scared – but once I knew it was Mommy I was fine..."

"Dad said he was goin' to get his wife – he didn't give a fuck!" Anthony laughed...

"Damn right!" Titus said as he pulled Denise into a hug...

"Once I saw you – I knew I was good..."

"That's right..." Titus breathed as he pulled her into a kiss...

"Umm... hello? I'm still on the phone..." Rose yelled through the speaker...

"So!" Denise laughed...

"I'm comin' over..." she said and then she hung up...

"Girl – what happened?" Rose asked as she walked in without knocking...

"Hello to you too..." Titus laughed...

"C'mon y'all – sit down – I'll tell you what happened..." she said as she went over to the kitchen table and sat down...

"I'll make coffee..." Titus said as he went over to the cabinet and took cups down...

"Thank you baby..." Denise said...

"Hurry up!" Rose laughed...

"Le'me get a soda..." Anthony said as he went over to the refrigerator, took out a ginger ale, and sat at the table. Titus made coffee for everyone else, brought the cups to the table, and then he sat down...

"Okay..." Denise said and then she picked up her coffee and took a sip... "So I went to visit Mommy like I always do, I sat down, I leaned back, and I started reading Beauties book..."

"You must've been tired..." Malexus said...

"I was – but I didn't think I'd fall asleep..."

"Damn girl – was the book that good?" Rose asked...

"Oh it's good – but let me tell you what happened – so I woke up – I was about to get up – and girl..."

"What?" Rose asked...

"Them zombies were moanin'... and fuckin'!"

"Ma!" Anthony exclaimed...

"Boy stop – how you think you got here?" Titus laughed...

"Are you serious?" Rose asked...

"Girl yes! I tried to get up and Mommy pulled me back down!"

125

"Wait... wait... wait... Mommy pulled you back down?"

"Grandma came up out the ground?" Malexus asked...

"It happened so fast – I didn't know who she was – she put her hand over my mouth and sshhed me!"

"Oh hell no – 'xcuse my language..." Anthony said...

"Your mother put her hand over your mouth?" Titus asked...

"Yes she did – at first I told her get off me – but once I knew who she was – I did like she told me!" Denise laughed...

"I know this is crazy... but imagine if you saw Mommy fuckin'?" Rose laughed...

"Oh my God – I'm leaving!" Malexus exclaimed as she got up and left the table and Titus bust out laughing.

Excerpt from Erotic Zombies 2

"Della – I'm standing here with Brooke Bethea. We're at the New Stratford Motor Inn in Stratford, which is directly across the street from St. Michael's Cemetery – go ahead Brooke – tell us what you saw..."

"Oh my God – I came out my room to get some ice – I heard this moaning – at first I thought it was people in the room next door because these walls are paper thin – so after I got my ice I was going back to my room and I looked across the street and let me tell you..."

"Go ahead Brooke..."

"They we're going crazy! I took my phone out to record it and I was like – what the fuck are they doing?"

"What were they doing?"

"They were running all around the cemetery, knocking over tombstones, and fuckin'! – Oh – 'xcuse my language..."

"That's okay – Della – I'm crossing the street and moving closer to the cemetery – can you see what's going on in there?"

"I sure can – if it wasn't for the gate, they might be in the street..."